Dearest, Loveliest Elizabeth

PRIDE & PREJUDICE
Continues

Dearest, Loveliest Elizabeth

ISBN-13: 978-1519790811

ISBN-10: 1519790813

Acknowledgments

What a pleasure it has been fashioning this account of what might have happened after the happily-ever-after ending of Jane Austen's timeless classic, *Pride and Prejudice.* Special thanks to Ken and Betty for all that you do.

Table of Contents

"Happy for all her maternal feelings was the day on which Mrs. Bennet got rid of her two most deserving daughters.

With what delighted pride she afterwards visited Mrs. Bingley, and talked of Mrs. Darcy, may be guessed."

Jane Austen

Chapter 1

The Means of Uniting

I am the happiest creature in the world, Elizabeth Darcy née Bennet considered, in joyful remembrance of having written those words in a missive to her aunt Mrs. Gardiner so many months ago. She had completed her sentiments by writing, *Perhaps other people have said so before, but not one with such justice. I am happier even than Jane. She only smiles, I laugh.*

By his own account the happiest man in the world, Fitzwilliam Darcy, a tall, handsome man with chiseled features and noble mien, soon joined his wife outside. He breathed in the fresh morning air. How she loved this man. What a pleasure it was to awaken each morning knowing his was the first face she would see. Positioning his warm body behind her, he wrapped his arms around her waist and bestowed soft kisses along her neckline. "I knew I'd find you here," he said at length.

His warm breath against her skin comforted her. She smiled. "I declare this is a most delightful view of the rising sun. I do not know that I shall ever tire of it." Being alone with her husband on the balcony overlooking a small, glistening pond and witnessing the dawn of a new day was becoming one of Elizabeth's favorite morning rituals. Nestled comfortably in his arms, his lips gently trailing along her skin and his fingers intertwined with hers, she could not imagine a better moment.

Darcy said, "Pray what are you thinking, my love?"

"I merely recalled my reply to a letter from Aunt Gardiner in which she endeavored to remind me of all your good qualities."

"No one can deny your aunt's impeccable taste. I owe a great deal of my happiness to her as well as your uncle, for in bringing you with them during their tour of the North, I must credit them for providing the means of uniting us."

A warm feeling washed over Elizabeth in the wake of this glowing commendation of two people so dear to her heart. Her spirits rising to playfulness, she said, "Let us not forget to acknowledge your own aunt, Lady Catherine de Bourgh, as well, for if I recall correctly, her confrontation with me in Hertfordshire over wild speculations that you and I were to be married is what taught you to hope that a union between us was even possible."

During the aforementioned incident, Lady Catherine de Bourgh, who hailed from Kent, had been extremely indignant about her nephew's marriage. In keeping with the frankness of her character, she announced her opposition to the scheme in a scathing letter with exceedingly abusive language, especially of Elizabeth.

"Granted, except I do not imagine I shall ever be able to thank her properly as she has cut all ties with us."

"You will be censured, slighted, and despised by everyone connected with him. Your alliance will be a disgrace; your name will never even be mentioned by any of us," said Elizabeth in a tone disconcertingly similar to the grand lady. She laughed a little. "Thank Heavens her dire prognostications did not prove true."

If there was one thing Elizabeth knew about her husband's haughty aunt, it was that she did not like to be proved wrong. This must certainly explain the lady's lapse in extending an invitation to her favorite nephew to visit her palatial home in Kent during Easter. Not that Elizabeth minded the slight. The last thing she wanted or needed was harsh disparagement from someone in whose home she might be a guest.

Darcy kissed his wife's earlobe. "Joy, contentment, and perfect harmony have been our constant companions from the moment we met at the altar."

"Indeed," Elizabeth said smilingly. She threw a reflective glance over all that had unfolded since she accepted Darcy's second proposal last autumn until the present. First, there was their courtship period during which she'd spent as much time shielding him from the ridiculousness of her Hertfordshire family and acquaintances as she'd spent getting to know more about him. Next came the wedding, their first Christmas as husband and wife spent with his noble relations in Matlock, the months-long wedding journey in the south of England, and finally her presentation at court during her first, albeit abbreviated, Season in town. The time had finally arrived for her to assume her proper place among Derbyshire society as the wife of one of the wealthiest men in the county.

Elizabeth and Pemberley's esteemed housekeeper, Mrs. Reynolds, had spent prodigious time planning the occasion that would include an elaborate dinner party for her husband's peers and their wives, as well as a separate celebration for the tenants. Both events were of equal importance to Elizabeth. Her reputation as the mistress of Pemberley was at stake as well as Darcy's reputation for having chosen his wife either wisely or poorly.

Elizabeth had insisted on inviting her sister Jane and Jane's husband, Charles Bingley. Indeed, she could not imagine taking on such a monumental feat without her dearest sister by her side. She invited the Gardiners as well. She did not extend an invitation to her other relatives. Her lapse was by design. It vexed her that the Bingley party included Miss Caroline Bingley, the younger of Charles' two sisters. The young woman spent the better part of her time in London with the older Bingley sister, Mrs. Louisa Hurst, but, as fate would have it, she was staying at Netherfield when the invitation to come to Pemberley was extended. The situation of her being at Pemberley during such an important time for the Darcys could have been far worse had both of Bingley's sisters been there. Elizabeth consoled herself as best she could with the knowledge that the absence of one half of the pernicious duo always rendered the other half rather more tolerable.

Sighing over the prospect of surrendering her idyllic spot, Elizabeth squeezed her husband's hand, and then moved to go inside. Too much needed doing if she planned to have breakfast with her family who might soon begin stirring.

"You're not leaving me already are you, my love?"

"I must discuss the seating arrangements with Mrs. Reynolds. Then I have planned to sit with Mrs. Garrison to go over the menus for the dinner party as well as the banquet. Lest you forget, no sooner will the formal dinner party be over and the overnight guests taken their leave than the tenant festivities we have planned commence. After meeting with Mrs. Garrison, I must visit the conservatory to speak with Mr. Spanks about the floral arrangements." Elizabeth placed her fingers to her lips. "Why do I feel as though I am neglecting something?"

Darcy said, "Because you are—something vital…"

Elizabeth arched her brow inquiringly.

"Your husband," he said playfully. "Can't all those other matters wait awhile longer?"

"Why? What do you have in mind?"

Darcy took her hand, raised it to his lips, and brushed a kiss over her knuckles. Lowering it, he started guiding her into the house.

"Where are you leading me?"

"Where do you think?" Darcy's eyes tore away from his wife toward the direction of their bed.

"As much as I would enjoy the prospect of lingering in bed, I am afraid I cannot. I have so much to do this morning."

"I assure you, my dearest, loveliest Elizabeth, there will be no lingering this morning. That is unless you consider this lingering." He swept her into his arms and kissed her lips passionately. At length, he ceased. "Or this," he whispered, lowering her to their bed. "I dare say anything else that you have planned for this morning can wait."

Gazing into his wife's eyes, he stripped himself of the shirt and trousers he had casually donned earlier and slid into bed beside her. Affectionately taking her into his arms, Darcy commenced doing all the things to Elizabeth that a woman wanted her lover to do.

Indeed, Mrs. Elizabeth Darcy could not be happier.

~~~

The atmosphere at Pemberley took a decided turn later that day. Elizabeth ought to have known her mother would look upon the occasion of Pemberley's first formal dinner party as a chance to get rid of her remaining unmarried daughters, Mary and Kitty, by throwing them in the path of wealthy men of Darcy's ilk. Indeed, fewer than two days after the Bingleys and the Gardiners arrived, Elizabeth's Longbourn relations descended upon Pemberley's doorstep.

She was not entirely surprised to see her father, Mr. Thomas Bennet, arrive unannounced, for he delighted in coming to Pemberley, especially when he was least expected. As familiar as he was with the house, he had made his way straight to the library where she suspected he would remain for the better part of his visit.

Having refreshed themselves after their journey and now brightly attired in a rainbow of soft colors, Mrs. Fanny Bennet, Mary, who was next in age after Elizabeth, and Kitty, who was next to Mary, joined the Darcys, the Bingleys, and the Gardiners in the parlor. An amiable, intelligent, elegant woman, and a great favorite with all her nieces, Mrs. Gardiner was immediately surrounded by Kitty and Mary: the former impatient to hear all there was to hear about the newest fashions, and the latter eager to learn which books she ought to read next. Mrs. Bennet contented herself with a steady stream of questions on the topic of who would be attending Elizabeth's grand dinner party. *How many of the guests are gentlemen? Are any of them single? Are they rich?*

Such conversation, it seemed, was the order of the day and Elizabeth began to consider that her family's being there was not the worst thing that could happen. Indeed, it was rather nice to see the faces of so many of the people whom she loved in one place, sitting and talking, enjoying one another's company. She even supposed that perhaps she ought to have invited them. It had been far too long since they had all been together—not since her nuptials. Who was to say when next they would see each other again. No sooner had she accustomed herself to this notion than the butler, Mr. Thurman, entered the room.

The tall, austere man cleared his throat. "Mrs. Lydia Wickham," he announced. In a flash, Elizabeth's youngest sister swept into the parlor. A quiet hush overtook everyone assembled about. Mary, who had moved to sit off by herself in a corner, looked up from her book long enough to nod a less than enthusiastic greeting to her sister. Lydia's own exuberance earned the highest admiration of the sister who was next to her in age. Kitty, a pretty, brown-haired young lady with bright eyes and a quizzical smile, giggled with excitement.

Mrs. Bennet's joy in seeing her favorite daughter for the first time since shortly after the latter had married was beyond expression, and her spirits were immediately heightened. She was never quite as lively as she was when in company with her youngest. The merry matriarch sprang to her feet and tore across the room.

"Oh, Lydia, my dear, it is such a happy surprise to see you! Turn around and let me have a look at you!"

Lydia was a stout, well-grown young woman with a fine complexion and friendly countenance. A favorite with her mother, whose affection had brought her into public at an early age, she had high animal spirits and a sort of natural self-consequence that had only been encouraged by the fact that, although the youngest, she had been the first of the five Bennet daughters to be married. The particulars of how said marriage came to be never concerned her. Relishing in her mother's unabashed adoration, Lydia spun herself around in a proud manner.

Mrs. Bennet clasped her hands to her chest. "I can easily surmise that your dashing husband is taking prodigious care of you." Winking, she added, "You were very clever in landing such a handsome man. No doubt he spoils you exceedingly were one to judge by your elegant dress and your fine jewels."

The proud matriarch was not alone in noticing Lydia's lavish attire. Elizabeth could not help silently noting her sister's extravagance as well. During the past months, such relief as it was in her power to afford, by the practice of thrifty economy in her own private expenses, she frequently sent to the Wickhams. It had always been evident to her that such an income as theirs, under the direction of two people so excessive in their wants and heedless of the future, must be insufficient to their support. Her benevolence aside, she decided it was best not to judge her sister on the basis of this one factor alone. *Who is to say this is not the only such gown my sister owns?*

"Just imagine; you are happily married to an officer! There was a time when I should have loved to have married an officer, but then I met your father and there was the end of that dream." She looked around the room. "Where is our dear Wickham? Pray you did not travel all this way alone, child! Where is your excellent husband?"

"Oh, Mama! I assure you that my Wickham and I did indeed travel to Derbyshire together. He is in Lambton—that dreadful little town. When last I saw him, he was settling into a dreary little room in a tiny little inn. Oh, if only you could have seen the place, then you would have known in an instant that it is no place for the sister of one of the richest men in all of Derbyshire. I told the innkeeper as much, and I insisted he must give us the finest rooms in the establishment, but he would not hear of it. Oh, Mama, you will never guess what he did. Well, I will tell you what he did and save you the trouble."

"Do tell, my dear," cried Mrs. Bennet when she could.

"I told him that if he fails to heed my demands that we shall take our patronage elsewhere and he said that he could not and, what's more, he would not even if he could—complaining of having been ill-used by my dear Wickham in the past, but that was ages ago."

"My dear Lydia, why did Wickham not come with you to stay at Pemberley? No doubt there is ample room."

Darcy had heard enough. "George Wickham is not welcome at Pemberley," he said in a tone that invited no further discussion on the matter.

Not easily put off by the absence of an invitation as evidenced by her even being at Pemberley, Mrs. Bennet exclaimed, "Not welcome at Pemberley! Why, I have never heard of such a thing." She looked away from the master of the house and turned her aggrieved gaze to the mistress. "When is it ever proper to exclude one's own family from one's home? Why, I should never dream of turning family away. Did I not welcome that horrible Mr. Collins and his scheming wife, the former Miss Charlotte Lucas, at Longbourn? We all know I took no pleasure in doing so, but family is family. We are not allowed the privilege of picking and choosing those whom we like best."

"Those are my sentiments exactly, Mama," cried Lydia. "However, I am not angry and neither is my Wickham. In fact, he told me to be sure to give his best wishes to Mr. and Mrs. Darcy and most especially to Miss Georgiana." Lydia threw a casual glance about the room, dismissing everyone she knew until her eyes landed on someone whose acquaintance she had not made. She sashayed over to where Georgiana was standing and curtseyed. "You must be Miss Darcy. My Wickham said you were a comely creature. No doubt my sisters have told you all about me and how I was the first Bennet daughter to marry. I am quite eager to further our acquaintance, for I am certain you and I have much in common."

The discomfort that Miss Darcy felt in the wake of all the talk of Wickham was plain for her brother to see. Having more than her fair share of elegance, the accomplished young woman could do no more than smile awkwardly at Lydia's unseemliness while saying nothing in response.

Darcy had really had enough by now and, rather than continue to expose himself to such flagrant lack of decorum, he left the room with not even a by your leave.

Chapter 2

Awe and Approbation

Darcy never liked Mrs. Wickham. He fought against cursing himself for providing the means of that silly girl boasting of having such an appellation. His sentiments toward Mrs. Bennet were scarcely better. Their relationship had been marred with contention from the start. Darcy shuddered in recollection of some of the nasty exchanges between them during his first visit to Hertfordshire with his friend Bingley.

His thoughts immediately wandered to the day he arrived at Longbourn after he spoke to Mr. Bennet of his wish to marry Elizabeth. The next day, Mrs. Bennet's behavior toward him had been decidedly different—marked with awe and approbation.

Their mutual endeavors at civility during Darcy's subsequent visits to Longbourn aside, he could not say he would ever do anything more than tolerate his mother-in-law. True, her decided admiration toward him was always on display when she had nothing better to do with her time and no one to give her cause to lament her fondest complaints. However, there were too many times when she would be vulgar. Her sister from Meryton, Mrs. Philips, always brought out the worst in her and so did her youngest daughter, he now recalled.

The next couple of days – Heaven forbid, weeks – will surely test my patience.

He suffered a pang of empathy for what his sister Georgiana must have suffered what with Lydia's constant mentioning of that vile husband of hers. He made a mental note to speak with her. Pemberley now being Georgiana's home, her attachment with Elizabeth was exactly what Darcy had hoped to see. Lydia may be his wife's sister, but he would be damned if he allowed that silly girl to injure Georgiana. *If Lydia's being at Pemberley is a source of discomfort for my sister then Lydia must leave.*

Darcy was pacing the floor when Elizabeth entered the room.

Approaching him, she demanded, "Could you have been any ruder toward my mother and sister?"

"I suppose I might have stayed in the room and told them what I truly thought of their ill-mannered display, so, yes, I could have been ruder." He ran his fingers through his dark hair. "What on Earth are those two about? It is as though they are determined to make themselves ridiculous wherever they go."

"I fear you are too severe on my mother and Lydia. They have no premeditated motives toward behaving ridiculously. They are the same as they ever were, and their exhibitions are merely exaggerated as a consequence of their being parted for so long."

"And this must be their excuse for such vulgarity in the presence of others. Would that they simply remove themselves from the company of the civilized members of our party, and then no one would have any cause to repine—especially me."

She pursed her lips. "As much as I respect them, I believe I thought only of you." Elizabeth folded one arm over the other. "Those were your words, sir, not mine. Did you really mean what you said that day or was it merely a clever way of ingratiating yourself with me at the time? And if you did indeed mean every word you said then what happened?"

"What happened? What happened was the spectacle your mother and your youngest sister have made of themselves almost from the moment of their arrival. That is what happened! Am I expected to rejoice in the fact that my sister must be reminded of that vile George Wickham at every turn?"

"Perhaps you ought to have thought of that before you married me!"

"Perhaps I should have!"

Taken aback, Elizabeth gasped at his declaration. Darcy could have no doubt of the impact of his words upon his lady. He felt just as horrible having uttered them. He could never regret their union. Angry people did not always think before speaking. Surely this was the case now.

"Please forgive me, Elizabeth. You know I did not mean a word of what I just said. It is just that it pains me every time that scoundrel's name is mentioned in front of Georgiana. True, I blame myself, but not enough to regret our marriage. I love you more than life itself. Tell me you know that."

"Indeed, I do, sir. How could I deny it? You prove your love for me every day. Pray do not think for one moment that I am impervious to what the mention of his name must do to Georgiana. Do not forget that she is my sister too. I feel her pain most acutely, and I wish more than anything that there was something I might do to temper my mother and Lydia's high praises of the man. In their defense, they know nothing of the history of Wickham and your family other than what he may have told them."

"I hope you understand why I prefer to keep it that way. Other than you, I have told no one. As Richard is my sister's co-guardian," he said, referring to his cousin Colonel Fitzwilliam, "he knows of course. He and I do not speak on the matter—neither do Georgiana and I for that matter. Heaven only knows what havoc would be wrought on my sister's prospects were it to be made widely known what happened in Ramsgate." He looked at her with eyes begging reassurance. "You've not mentioned a word of it to anyone, have you? Not even Jane?"

She hesitated a little. "I must confess that, in enlightening Jane of Wickham's true character as described in your letter, I repeated the whole of its contents so far as they concerned him. I assure you that you may rely upon my sister's discretion."

Darcy colored a little. "What of the letter? Is it in a safe and secure place, or did you heed my advice and burn it?"

"Indeed, I eventually burned it. Although I confess that I hesitated a little before doing so."

"I fail to see why. It was, after all, written in a dreadful bitterness of spirit."

"The letter, perhaps, began in bitterness, but it did not end so. The adieu was charity itself." Those words would forever be impressed upon her mind.

I will only add, God bless you. Fitzwilliam Darcy

Recalling herself to her purpose, Elizabeth said, "Pray let us not dwell on those matters from the past that give us both displeasure and rather focus upon the issue at hand. My family is here now, and it seems they are to remain here for the foreseeable future. I will be seriously displeased should you afford my relations the same callous disregard as you evidenced this evening."

"I shall make no such promise other than I will do my best. With that said, can we simply pretend that I did not walk unceremoniously out of the room on your mother and sister? Better still, let us pretend that she and Mrs. Wickham"— he nearly spat the appellation— "are not even here, if only for tonight? There are far more pleasant endeavors for us to entertain. Do you not agree?"

His less than contrite manner was not at all in accordance with the severity of his offense, Elizabeth felt. "You cannot be serious, sir."

"Indeed, I am. You know how much I dislike the prospect of retiring to bed angry." He took her hands in his and kissed both of them in their turn. "Please, let us not allow family matters to come between us."

"If family matters should come between us, it will not be my doing."

"It sounds as though you mean to abdicate yourself entirely from the task of reining in your mother and your sister."

Elizabeth released an exasperated sigh. "It has been a long day, and I am far too tired to continue talking over the matter at this time. Perhaps you and I might take up this discussion in the morning. Shall we meet in the breakfast parlor before the others have awakened?" she asked in a tone that suggested that his sharing her bed was not an option.

"What became of our wedding night edict not to go to bed angry? Have you forgotten?"

"No—I haven't forgotten."

He kissed her forehead. "Good, because I believe you were the one who suggested it."

"I am nothing if not a woman of my word. But that is not to say I will not fall asleep the moment my head touches the pillow," she said and then added a healthy yawn for good measure.

Darcy walked behind his wife and began sprinkling soft kisses along her slender neckline. "That, my dearest, loveliest Elizabeth, remains to be seen."

~~~

Early the next day, Elizabeth and her eldest sister were out for a walk. Her sister's calm serenity was just the diversion Elizabeth needed. "Jane," she began, "I always suspected you were a true angel. Now I have irrefutable proof."

"Dearest Lizzy, to what do I owe such high praise?"

"Owe it to the fact that you have managed to live so close to Longbourn – to Mama – and you have not succumbed to madness. Mama has been here for less than a full day, and I am at my wits' end."

"Trust me, Lizzy, I am unworthy of such admiration. The truth is that Charles and I have been secretly plotting our escape from Hertfordshire for months. Nothing would bring us more joy than to be settled nearby to you and Darcy. That is but one of the reasons we plan to stay on after the festivities. Charles intends to speak with Darcy and solicit his help in locating a suitable estate here in Derbyshire."

"Oh! That is the best thing I could have possibly heard. I should love it."

"It pleases me that you are delighted with the news, for I should hate to think that our residing in such proximity to Pemberley would be a cause for displeasure."

"I do not suppose Mama will be pleased to be robbed of the satisfaction of knowing one of her daughters is the mistress of Netherfield."

"Nor will Kitty be happy to lose her favorite prospective venue for balls. We have yet to give one, as you know, even though it's Kitty's most earnest request."

Elizabeth could well imagine what Jane said was true. Every letter she received from Kitty gave the strongest hints of her ardent desire for Elizabeth to have a grand ball at Pemberley as well. She sighed inside. *Perhaps one day I shall, but for now it is all I can do to accustom myself to my new home and all my responsibilities as the mistress of such a grand estate and wife of one of the wealthiest men in the county.*

Elizabeth said, "To Papa's credit, he remains steadfast in his resolve to keep her safe from the great disadvantage of the Wickhams' society by never consenting to allow her to accept Lydia's frequent invitations to come and stay with her, with the promise of balls and young men."

"Indeed, but I am given to consider that it would be to Kitty's material advantage were she to spend the chief part of her time away from Meryton. In another society she would improve significantly in both temperament and understanding. I should hope that wherever Charles and I live she will be a frequent guest."

"Once again, dearest Jane, you have proved to be a true angel. Indeed, I shall follow your example in that regard." Here again, Elizabeth's mind wandered to Kitty's desire for a ball at Pemberley. Even if she wanted to give a ball, she did not know how her husband would feel. A grand dinner party was one thing, it suited his idea of how members of civilized society ought to spend their time; a ball was another matter altogether. In all the time she had known him he had not shown any particular interest in attending such gatherings. *How would he fare were he prevailed upon to host one?*

"No doubt Mary will be displeased over the loss of Charles' ever-expanding library," said Jane, piercing Elizabeth's thoughts.

Elizabeth nodded. "Then there's the matter of Caroline's displeasure. She likes to boast of her eager disdain of Meryton and its small society, but that does not seem to dissuade her from being a frequent guest."

"Lizzy, I know you may not enjoy hearing this, but my sister is quite changed."

Elizabeth supposed the young woman liked to pretend she had changed. Indeed, she had gone out of her way to pay off every arrear of civility toward Elizabeth since the wedding, but Elizabeth thought she knew better. A leopard did not change its spots so easily as that, and she had seen the manner in which Caroline's well-practiced smile turned into a sneer whenever she thought no one was looking. Although that young woman was fonder than ever of Georgiana and almost as attentive to Darcy, Elizabeth smiled in spite of herself for the unflattering image her mind conjured of Caroline circling Pemberley like a vulture hoping for Elizabeth to keel over at any moment so that she might swoop down and feast upon the spoils.

"Jane, you have always been the one who only saw the good in everyone. However, I thought your eyes had been awakened to Caroline's true character long ago."

"No doubt you are speaking of the lengths to which she and certain others, whose names I dare not mention, went to separate Charles and me."

Elizabeth always wondered if Bingley had confided Darcy's role in the scheme to Jane. It seemed he had if Jane's last words were an indication. The very thought of what he had done and the heated words between them when she had found out pained her still.

"I have every reason in the world to think ill of you. No motive can excuse the unjust and ungenerous part you acted there. You dare not, you cannot deny that you have been the principal, if not the only means of dividing them from each other—of exposing one to the censure of the world for caprice and instability, and the other to its derision for disappointed hopes, and involving them both in misery of the acutest kind." Having paused and detected in him not a single shred of remorse, but rather a smile of affected incredulity, she repeated, "Can you deny that you have done it?"

With assumed tranquillity he then replied, "I have no wish of denying that I did everything in my power to separate my friend from your sister, or that I rejoice in my success. Toward him I have been kinder than toward myself."

Elizabeth shook her head to chase away the memory. She had forgiven Darcy and Bingley had too. Surely it was not in her sister's nature to fail to do likewise.

"Jane—"

"Lizzy, I think I know what you are about to say. I assure you that I suffer no ill will toward anyone as a consequence of what happened then. In this regard, I say we adhere to your philosophy to remember the past only as it brings one pleasure." Reaching out to touch and squeeze her hand, she smiled warmly. "What say you, my dearest sister?"

Elizabeth's spirits quickly rose to playfulness. She chuckled. "Who am I to argue in the face of such sage advice?"

Meanwhile, Darcy and Bingley were set to embark on a similar discussion. The two had just enjoyed a vigorous race on horseback across one of Pemberley's expansive open fields and were walking back to the stables, leading their mounts by their respective reins.

The events of the past evening weighed heavily on Darcy's busy mind, as did the thought of how his friend must suffer being at Netherfield—three miles away from Longbourn. "Bingley, how do you do it?"

The younger man, who also appeared a bit distracted, pursed his lips. "How do I do what, Darcy?"

"How do you survive your mother-in-law day in and day out? I can well imagine she fancies Netherfield an extension of her own home."

Bingley laughed at his friend's assertion. "I endure it far better than you, I am afraid. However, has that not always been the way of it so far as you and our mother-in-law are concerned?"

"I take it you are referring to all those times she took umbrage at me while I was visiting you at Netherfield when she insinuated that I lacked good breeding. I believe her exact words were, 'That is my idea of good breeding, and those persons who fancy themselves very important, and never open their mouths, quite mistake the matter'," Darcy said mockingly.

Bingley laughed a little at this rarely exhibited side of his friend. "Ah, and that is but one of several occasions, if I recall correctly. Your disagreements were ones for the history books."

"I do not know that I would go so far as to suggest all that."

"No—I suppose I exaggerate a bit. However, one does reach a point at which having one's family nearby is more of an inconvenience than not. It is for that reason Jane and I plan to settle elsewhere."

"I understand it has long been a favorite wish of yours to purchase an estate. I commend you in having committed to the idea. Have you given a thought to where you should like to live?"

"Indeed, we are thinking of purchasing an estate in Derbyshire or hereabouts. It would be a fine thing if you would accompany me to look at some of the places of interest. I plan to do things correctly this time around. Not that I regret my hastiness in letting Netherfield Park, mind you, for that turned out to be one of the best decisions of my life."

Which is to say nothing of how my own life changed for the better as well, Darcy thought.

"Our decision on where we shall reside will affect the rest of our lives. It is to be the place where we raise our children, where our children raise their children, and so on for generations to come."

Darcy could not have been more pleased by this intelligence. His friend had inherited property to the amount of nearly a hundred thousand pounds from his father, who had intended to purchase an estate himself but did not live to do it. There was the expectation that Bingley planned to do likewise. At times, he even decided on a county. Once he let Netherfield, however, Darcy suspected he might easily spend the remainder of his days there, what with the easiness of his temper, and simply leave the next generation to purchase. Darcy was indeed delighted to hear Bingley speaking this way. He told him as much.

"Bingley, I cannot tell you what it means to me hearing you go on and on in this way. Marriage has done things to you and all for the better."

~~~

The balmy afternoon breeze afforded the perfect excuse for a ride around the park for two.

"I feel almost guilty stealing you away from the others," said Mrs. Gardiner to Elizabeth. "I am amazed you remember my remarking in my tell-all letter about how a low phaeton with a nice little pair of ponies would be the very thing, for I was merely speaking in jest."

A tell-all letter is precisely what it was. Elizabeth might never have learned about Mr. Darcy's relentless endeavor to recover her sister Lydia if her aunt had not been the one to tell her. Darcy truly did intend to keep his part in the scheme a secret. Indeed, Elizabeth had committed her aunt's letter to heart. It was a good thing, too, for time away from the manor house with her dearest aunt was just the thing she needed.

"A promise is a promise, is it not? Even one given tacitly."

"I suppose you are correct. As much as I am enjoying it, I would not wish to keep you away too long. No doubt you have an endless list of things to accomplish before the festivities begin."

"Indeed, I do. However, if I am to be completely honest, I would have to confess that Mrs. Reynolds is more than capable of handling everything without me. She was expertly overseeing the smooth operations of the manor house before I was even conceived."

"Pray, Lizzy, why would you say such a thing? You must not minimize your importance as mistress of

Pemberley. In the short time I have been here, I have seen the effect of your presence all around. Pemberley feels more like a home now than when we first visited. That is to say nothing of the change in your husband. Anyone who's ever had the good fortune of being in love need only observe the way he looks at you to know he loves you deeply."

"The question is will he love me just as deeply by the time Mama and Lydia are done making a complete spectacle of themselves?"

"Oh, dear, pray the two of you are not suffering any discord as a consequence of my sister Bennet and young Lydia."

"You observed the manner in which he stormed out of the room the other day, did you not?"

"Yes, it seems the mention of Mr. Wickham's name is rather disconcerting for him and his sister."

"Dearest Aunt, if only you knew the extent of my husband's grievances against that man whom I must now call my brother."

"I rather suspected the history between those two gentlemen was marred with contentiousness when we were all in London preparing for the wedding that Lydia is so fond of boasting of. I know none of the particulars, nor would I ever wish to, for it can hardly be any of my concern, but I will tell you this. If all that Darcy endured in seeing the Wickham affair settled did not diminish his ardent esteem for you, then nothing on this earth ever will."

Chapter 3

Put Asunder

Lydia, Georgiana, Mary, and Kitty were walking about the lanes when Lydia impatiently seized Georgiana's arm. "Come, Georgiana, let us walk ahead of the others for I should like my fair share of your attention."

Despite feeling the young woman's rudeness toward the others, Georgiana silently consented. When they were a few paces ahead of their party, Lydia said, "My sisters, Mary and Kitty, had the pleasure of making your acquaintance at Lizzy's wedding. I should have liked to have been there, and I would have been there too had Lizzy prevailed upon Darcy to make the proper arrangements, which I am certain he would have done given everything else he did for me and my dear Wickham."

"I beg your pardon," cried Georgiana.

"Oh, I should not have said a word, for that is meant to be a great secret. Pray forget I said anything."

Georgiana's countenance clouded a bit, but she said nothing.

Lydia said, "It is a fine morning for a walk, is it not?"

"Indeed, it is."

"I always enjoyed walking with my sisters when we were all at Longbourn. Hardly a day went by, weather permitting, that we did not venture to Meryton. Do you ever walk to Lambton?"

"I am afraid I do not. Even if I wished it, my brother would never hear of such a thing."

"I suppose it is very far when I am forced to think of it. Meryton is a very easy distance from my father's estate. And, as I said, my sisters and I so enjoyed walking there—Lizzy especially, for she has always been an excellent walker. Did you know that on one of our walks to Meryton we had the pleasure of meeting Mr. Wickham for the first time?"

Georgiana's voice cracked a little. "I did not."

"Indeed. How fortunate we thought ourselves at the time, although I am forced to confess that he only noticed Lizzy and she likewise took note of him. He was her favorite beau for the longest time, but then a Miss Mary King —who went away to Liverpool once she inherited a small fortune —stole him away from Lizzy. That freckled thing—what Wickham admired about her

I can scarcely imagine. However, as I said, she went away, which delighted all the other ladies in Meryton exceedingly and no one more than me, for I became the happy woman toward whom he lavished all his adoration from then on, and the rest, as they say, is history." Lydia shrugged. "I say 'as they say' although, for the life of me, I have not a clue who *they* are."

Georgiana did not utter anything in reply. Her mind was frantically engaged in thought on the implications of Lydia's speech. She wondered if her brother knew of Elizabeth's early fondness for George Wickham. *If perchance he did then how did he endure it?*

Lydia tugged at Georgiana's sleeve to reclaim her attention. "Why does your brother not allow my Wickham to visit Pemberley? We are all family are we not?"

"No doubt my brother has what he supposes is a valid reason."

"I'll tell you his reason. It is because Darcy is so very mean. Why, you would think he would welcome both of us with open arms given that he paid for my own wedding and Wickham's commission." Lydia slapped her hand over her mouth. "Oh," she cried, "there I go again telling the world what is meant to be a secret, but I trust I may depend on you not to tell another living soul, and I shall endeavor to do the same."

"You may depend on it," Georgiana said tentatively, not entirely convinced she would keep her word. *Why would my brother do such a thing?*

"Well, as I was saying, not only is Darcy mean-spirited when it comes to my Wickham, I fear he is exceedingly jealous, for everyone liked my Wickham best when we made his acquaintance in Hertfordshire and not a single one of us could tolerate Darcy—not even Lizzy." Lydia huffed. "La! Especially not Lizzy!" she exclaimed. "She hated him the most. Of course, one would never know that now. The two of them forgave each other. Oh, if only they were half as magnanimous where my darling Wickham is concerned."

Georgiana pursed her lips in puzzlement. "I find it hard to believe that my brother and Elizabeth were ever at odds."

Lydia's mouth flew open. "You need not take my word for it," she said in the face of Georgiana's skepticism. "Ask Mary for she never lies. She always tells the truth." The young ladies turned to see what had become of the others. Kitty walked along with her arms crossed and her expression aggrieved. Mary trailed behind without regard to her surroundings with her head buried in a book.

"Oh, Mary!" Lydia cried. "Why are you reading on such a perfect day as this and at Pemberley of all places?"

Mary looked up at her sister inquisitively.

"Hurry and join us, for I want you to tell Georgiana how Darcy and Lizzy *really* felt about each other when they first met."

Mary adjusted her spectacles. "What God has joined together, let no man put asunder."

"La! Firstly, I am not a man, and secondly, I am not putting anything asunder. I speak nothing but the truth."

"Lydia!" Mary chastised. She and her youngest sister were as different as night and day. While the latter took pleasure in being the center of attention, the former preferred living in the shadows. Not only did she prefer it, she depended on it. The occasional comparison between her sisters' beauty and her own were becoming rather less mortifying with each passing day. She would not have traded places with any one of them. Her sisters might have suffered the greater part of their lives in fear of spinsterhood, but not Mary. Alas, with such a mother as Mrs. Bennet, whose business in life it was to see all her daughters well settled, Mary knew enough to keep her rather unconventional sentiments to herself.

Lydia hissed. "Oh, pay no attention to Mary. I am sure she means well, but everyone knows she is no fun. She would rather read a silly book than take notice of what is really important. Believe me when I say that everyone who knows anything about how your brother and my sister felt about each other during the earliest days of their acquaintance will tell you that he declared her barely tolerable and she proclaimed him the most arrogant and disdainful creature on Earth. Why, you can imagine how shocked I was when I learned that they were to be married and on the heels of my own wedding to my dear Wickham, which tells me that Lizzy simply could not bear the thought of having a younger sister married when she was on the verge of becoming an old spinster.

"I told her that I would be happy to help her and all my sisters find husbands, but she said she did not like my way of finding a husband. Although I am confident she would have been just as pleased with someone I picked out for her—" she paused to catch her breath "—except he would not have been nearly so rich as Darcy."

Lydia pressed her fingers to her lips. "La! I have a brilliant idea. What say we all go to Lambton tomorrow? It has been far too long since I had a new frock and I really must have something stunning to wear to the dinner party. Although, I would much rather my sister gave a ball. Oh! How I wish my Wickham were welcome at Pemberley for he would surely wear his red coat—he is ever so dashing in his red coat. Oh, but what am I saying? My Wickham could be dressed in a barrel and it would not make him one jot less handsome."

If Lydia had been looking, she might have noticed the color spread all over Georgiana's face. Lydia continued, "And we must ask Lizzy to join us, for she will be the one to pay for everything. To have a look at all this"—she waved her arms with astonishing flourish— "you would think my sister is the most selfish person in the world, for she hardly sends me any money at all—when she has so much and Wickham and I have so little."

Mary said, "It is entirely impolitic to discuss such matters, Lydia. Pray hold your tongue."

"Oh! Bother, Mary." She laced her arm through Georgiana's once again. "Are we not all family? Georgiana is our sister. I am sure there is nothing I would say to any of my sisters that I would not also say to her."

Later that day, Georgiana and Darcy were walking toward the stables. The two of them were planning a horseback riding excursion. Georgiana's mind was all aflutter after everything she had heard from Lydia earlier in the day. If half of what Lydia espoused was true, Georgiana suspected she never really knew her brother at all. Why had he condoned Elizabeth's sister marrying Mr. Wickham after his fierce opposition to an alliance between George and her? And what of all the earlier acrimony between her brother and Elizabeth; had Elizabeth's initial feelings for Wickham—the man who would be her brother's worst enemy—been the cause?

Darcy cleared his throat. "Georgiana, I saw you walking with Lydia today."

"Indeed, Kitty and Mary were walking with us as well."

"It appeared Lydia had a great deal to say."

"Though I have only just made her acquaintance, I feel confident in saying she is never at a lack for words."

Darcy tensed. He remained silent, which seemed to encourage his sister to continue.

"She seemed intent on regaling me with a thorough accounting of the earliest days of your acquaintance with Elizabeth. I never would have imagined they were marked with such strife—that there was a time the two of you did not even like each other."

The muscles stiffened in Darcy's shoulders. He wished his sister had not been an audience to such talk. As silly as Lydia was then and continued to be there was no telling how her ill-formed mind may have perceived things. From the moment he detected her wild behavior at the Meryton assembly to what he had thought would be the last he'd ever see of her at the Netherfield Ball, his opinion of her had gone steadily downhill.

Lydia's uncouth comportment gives proof to the reason that young girls ought not to come out when they are fifteen.

Now he could not even look at her without recalling the state in which he had found her living in squalor with that George Wickham. Nor was he likely ever to forget her appalling behavior in the days leading up to her wedding. All that he had done on Lydia's behalf he had done for Elizabeth. Having spent time with her at Pemberley, he did suffer a modicum of hope that Elizabeth might care for him. What unfolded during his subsequent visit to Longbourn with his friend Charles Bingley nearly put an end to that. The cool reception—bordering on incivility—he received from Elizabeth's mother was something to which he had accustomed himself. Elizabeth's lukewarm reception when he returned with Bingley was not what he had expected and had nearly persuaded him of her complete indifference. Had it not been for his aunt's timely visit to Longbourn on the heels of Bingley's proposal to Jane, he would have lost all hope forever.

Lady Catherine had called on him on her return through London. There, she related her journey to Longbourn, its motive, and the substance of her conversation with Elizabeth. His aunt had meant to secure Elizabeth's promise that she had not and never would accept a proposal of marriage from him. Unluckily for her ladyship, the visit's effect had been exactly contrariwise. It had taught him to hope as he had scarcely ever allowed himself to do theretofore. He knew enough of Elizabeth's disposition to be certain that, had she been absolutely and irrevocably decided against him, she would have acknowledged it to Lady Catherine, frankly and openly. This had been the basis for their good understanding that paved the way to their present happiness.

Darcy said, "Georgiana, I have never meant to give you the impression that my relationship with Elizabeth was without its share of trials and tribulations."

"No—I am not suggesting you did. However, I hope you will remember your own experiences when it comes to my own future acquaintances. I am very much aware that it was love that brought you and Elizabeth to where you are today. It was love that made you eschew society's expectations and commit to such an unequal alliance, and at the end of the day, it is love that will carry you through. I only ask that you will afford me the same level of understanding should I elect to follow my heart as well."

Chapter 4

The Intimate Nature

"What are your plans for today?" Elizabeth asked her husband the next morning.

"I will visit some of the tenants on the lower east side this morning. You should come with me."

"I rather supposed I would call on some of the tenants after the festivities."

"If that is what you feel is best. What do you plan to do today?"

"It seems I am to go into Lambton with Lydia. She said she needs to procure a few items for the dinner party."

Darcy arched his brow. "Will there be just the two of you?"

"Not exactly—I thought I would invite Georgiana, Kitty, and Mary to join us. We might make a day of it as it will require some time at the modiste."

"Again, you must do what you think is best. However, the possibility that Georgiana might be in proximity to George Wickham concerns me. I trust you will do everything in your power to prevent anything of that nature from happening." Darcy took a sip of his hot coffee. "It did not escape my notice that Lydia spent a prodigious amount of time chatting with Georgiana yesterday. There is no telling what she might have told her."

"Perhaps you would rather Georgiana and my sister Lydia kept their distance from each other as well."

"I have no wish to quarrel with you on this matter, Mrs. Darcy. Certainly, you can surmise that someone of Lydia's character is best kept away from impressionable young women. No doubt your father would agree with me. He would not wish to have Kitty or Mary spend time alone with Mrs. Wickham outside of supervision either." Darcy sat his paper aside. "If you feel uncomfortable with the position I am placing you in then simply bring Mrs. Annesley along with you to Lambton. She heeds my counsel without debate."

"Pardon me for thinking that you married me for reasons that have nothing in common with your reasons for engaging Mrs. Annesley's services, sir."

"Pray refrain from willfully misunderstanding me on this matter. It is just that Lydia is determined to plant seeds of discord in my sister's head that I fear are beginning to take root. That husband of hers may very well have put her up to her mischief making. All I ask is that you keep a sharp eye on the situation."

~~~

George Wickham sat alone for a time in a dimly lit corner of the room. He had made more enemies than not the last time he was in Derbyshire. The last thing he desired was someone to whom he owed money seeing him. Not to mention the degradation he suffered being the brother of *the* Fitzwilliam Darcy and yet being forced to stay in a shabby little inn.

Having finished the drink he'd been nursing for the past half hour, he was about to stand and quit the establishment when he saw a gentleman approaching his table. However, as best he could tell, he had never laid eyes on the man before that moment. What's more, the fellow was holding a bottle of liquor in one hand and balancing two glasses in the other.

I might as well see what this stranger is about, Wickham considered.

"May I offer you drink, sir—one weary traveler to another, as it were?"

Wickham gestured for the man to take a seat. "I do not see why not."

The man took the proffered seat. He sat the bottle and glasses down and extended his hand to Wickham. "Alston Carter, at your service."

"George Wickham," he returned, reaching not for the other man's hand, but the bottle. Wickham poured himself a drink and threw it back in short order. After making a face that testified to the quality of the liquor, he poured himself another. He looked at his new companion. "I must thank you for your generosity, good fellow."

"George Wickham, you say," the other man said.

"Indeed, no doubt you have heard of me. I believe I am a bit of a legend in these parts."

"Ah, but as I said, I am merely a weary traveler. I have been in Lambton for just a couple of days. Soon I will continue my travels."

"And where, pray tell, is your destination?"

The fellow shrugged. "I shall go wherever the road leads, good sir."

"Are you in search of anything in particular—a fortune or, heaven forbid, a woman?"

"That smacks of bitterness, my friend," said the other man who had by now poured himself a drink and was savoring its taste.

"I doubt there is anyone on Earth who would describe me as bitter," Wickham began. "Such is not in my nature, although if I were the type to suffer such sentiments, I would be wholly justified in doing so. My life, you see, is not at all what it was meant to be. I was destined to marry to a woman of means—with some sense and education—someone whose connections would have lifted me up. Yet, here I sit in this place on the outside wishing to be invited to my own childhood home—my family's home."

The other gentleman crossed one long leg over the other. "Family quarrels can be a tricky business, can they not?"

"You'll get no argument from me."

"You said you were meant to marry a woman of means. What happened to impede such a happy conclusion?"

Wickham threw back his drink in a single swallow. Wiping his mouth on his sleeve, he said, "Fitzwilliam Darcy is what happened."

"Pardon me, my friend, but do you speak of *the* Fitzwilliam Darcy of Pemberley?"

Wickham huffed. "Is there any other?"

"Might I ask what happened between the two of you?"

George Wickham was never one to shy away from a good Darcy lambasting, but, in this case, he was wary. How did he know this stranger was not one of Darcy's people? "I have said enough already." He looked up at the commotion at the door. "Ah, here is one of the greatest sources of my disappointment now."

The other man peered in the direction that Wickham was staring. "Pardon my saying so, but I see nothing at all to disappoint."

Wickham stood in hopes of garnering the ladies' attention. He gave his waistcoat a firm tug. "That is because you're not married to her."

"So, one of the ladies is Mrs. George Wickham. Which one is the lucky woman?"

"Mrs. Wickham is the one in red."

"And the other woman? What is her name?"

"That, my friend, is my sister—Mrs. Elizabeth Darcy."

Had Wickham been looking at the other man, he would have noticed the stranger's sudden discomfort; however, the former's attention was fixed on Lydia and Elizabeth, who had not yet seen him. "I am happy to introduce you—" Wickham began. Turning to look at his companion's face to see how the suggestion met with his approval, Wickham was surprised to find the gentleman was nowhere to be found. A quick glance at the glasses and the half-empty bottle on the table confirmed that he had not imagined the encounter. With that, he merely shrugged and set off in the ladies' direction.

Lydia raced to meet him as soon as she saw him. "Oh, my dear Wickham, you cannot possibly know how much I missed having you at my side all of last evening. The Darcys are ever so tedious!"

There was only one thing on Wickham's mind. "Did you have any success in garnering my acceptance at Pemberley?"

"I'm afraid I did not, but look! I did even better. I persuaded Lizzy to come with me to town, for you know

I am in dire need of a new frock to wear to her fancy dinner party. Now you may plead your own case. Come with me," she said. She grabbed his arm and started coaxing him along.

Elizabeth knew exactly what her sister Lydia was about. Cognizant of her husband's directive that Georgiana was not to spend a single second in Wickham's company, Elizabeth hastened to where the other ladies in her party were standing. Directing her speech to Mary, she said, "Please escort Georgiana and Kitty to the shop across the street and wait for me there. I shall be along shortly."

Mary's face reflected her joy at being useful to her sister. "Come along you two," she directed.

Kitty, having observed the Wickhams heading their way, protested. "Oh, must we leave? I should like very much to greet my brother. It has been ages since we last had the pleasure of his company at Longbourn."

"Do as I say at once," Elizabeth exclaimed with energy. She did not know if Georgiana suffered a similar opinion as Kitty, and she did not care. Mr. Darcy would be livid were she to ignore his wishes and allow Georgiana to remain in proximity while she exchanged forced pleasantries with her *brother*.

Some moments later, Elizabeth and Wickham stood opposite each other. This was their first meeting since the newly wedded Wickhams had traveled to Newcastle, although her purse was far lighter than it otherwise would have been if the Wickhams gave a care to moderation. It vexed her exceedingly that her sister's husband was the manner of man who would accept such charity in the first place. After greeting Wickham with measured civility, only one thing was uppermost in Elizabeth's mind. She meant to have it out with him for attempting to draw Georgiana into his scheme by way of Lydia. What she intended to discuss was not for Lydia's ears, else the whole world would learn of it. That he had not confided in his wife puzzled Elizabeth exceedingly, but of this she was certain for Lydia and secrets were always soon separated. She'd managed to keep the secret of Darcy being at the wedding for little to no time at all, Elizabeth recalled.

"Pray, Lydia, will you allow me a moment alone with your husband?"

"La! Why should I do that? I know how much you always liked him. How do I know I can trust you?"

Wickham took his wife's hand and brushed a kiss across her knuckles. "Pray do this for me, my darling wife."

She giggled. "Oh! You know I can never deny you anything."

Soon Lydia was gone, and it was just Elizabeth and Wickham standing in the middle of the floor. He swept a superfluous bow. "So, we meet again, dear Sister, albeit under circumstances that hardly befit the intimate nature of our acquaintance." Though Wickham strongly suspected that Elizabeth must now be acquainted with whatever of his ingratitude and falsehood had before been unknown to her, in spite of everything, he was not entirely without hope that Darcy might yet be prevailed upon to make his fortune.

Elizabeth shuddered inside at the thought of her once having believed this man was honorable. How gratified she was that, in spite of her initial preference for Wickham, her heart had never been truly touched by him. Fate had not been nearly so kind to her sister. Even now, Elizabeth felt a pang of guilt for not telling all her family about Wickham's true character once she discovered from Darcy what he was really like. All of them might have been spared such a disgusting connection.

"Sir, you and I are brother and sister owing to your marriage to my sister, and so it must be. However, I beg you not to insinuate there is the slightest bit of intimacy between us."

"What a shame it is to hear you speak this way. Do you deny that you and I were at one time very close—that we shared confidences the nature of which only the most intimate of acquaintances are wont to do? You may choose to forget, but I never shall. As a result, I have reserved a special place in my heart that is yours and yours alone," he said, laying his hand on his chest for effect.

Elizabeth frowned disapprovingly. "Pray remember yourself, sir."

"Is there another reason other than your desire to enjoy a few private moments with me that compelled you to ask your sister to leave us alone?"

"Indeed there is. I mean to tell you that both my husband and I are aware that you have set Lydia on a quest to create as much havoc at Pemberley as possible. I am here to tell you that it will not work and thus your efforts would be better spent elsewhere."

"I only mean to benefit from what is mine. Pemberley is my home. It is where I spent every day of my youth. How dare Darcy continue this foolish vendetta by banishing me from the only home I ever knew?"

"My husband has every right to insist you stay away from Pemberley, and you very well know it."

"Ah, but one word from you and he will most certainly change his mind," Wickham said.

"I have no wish to change his mind!"

"Perhaps you have been seduced by all the wealth and trappings of the man whom you once despised, and hence you have lost your once strong, independent will. Is that it? Has the officious, overbearing Fitzwilliam Darcy sapped you of your lively spirits? Or perhaps it is simply a matter of his not being in your power—perhaps he is not nearly so enthralled with his lovely wife as he supposed he would be. Knowing him as I do, no doubt he is disgusted to have so many Bennets swarming around his beloved Pemberley all at once." He leaned closer. "No doubt he married you thinking that, once he got you away from Hertfordshire, you would sever all ties with your former life."

"How my husband does or does not feel is none of your concern, sir. I demand you refrain from putting reprehensible ideas in my sister's head, else I shall know how to act." With that, Elizabeth turned to walk away.

Wickham stepped in front of her. Elizabeth's heartbeat sped up in pace. Her courage rising in the face of his attempt to intimidate her, she said, "Stand aside, sir." She walked to the part of the room where Lydia was standing in wait. "Unless you plan to remain here with your dear husband, Lydia, I suggest you bid him adieu this very moment and come along with me."

Lydia's resulting protests were wasted on Elizabeth, who kept walking. Surmising as much, Lydia relinquished all her anger toward her sister and fell in step behind her, for there was, after all, the matter of the new frock she so very much wanted. Her dear husband's cause could wait.

Chapter 5

Few and Far Between

Just when the Darcys believed things could not get any worse, they were the recipients of more uninvited guests. One of them was far more disagreeable now than when either of the Darcys had last seen her. This uninvited guest was none other than Darcy's aunt, Lady Catherine de Bourgh.

No sooner had she settled in the parlor than she commenced being silently outraged. Indeed, it was just as she had foretold. The shades of Pemberley had been thoroughly polluted. Her nephew Darcy wore the face of someone who was absolutely miserable and he had no one to blame but himself. Himself and his raging hormones, she silently pondered, for how else might one explain his decision to eschew his duties and responsibilities as well as society's expectation and commit to such an unequal alliance? Now he was the brother to the son of his late father's steward.

A tall, large woman, with strongly-marked features that might once have been handsome, Lady Catherine was confident that Darcy's late father would be appalled, despite his own misguided affinity for that wild George Wickham. She was certain her beloved sister, the late Lady Anne Darcy, would be equally appalled. For one thing, Lady Anne never did like George Wickham as a result of his meanness toward her only son, but more important than that was the fact that Lady Anne meant for her only son to marry her niece and namesake, Miss Anne de Bourgh—Lady Catherine's daughter.

In Mrs. Wickham, her ladyship saw little less than she always liked to suppose Darcy's wife to be: young and impertinent with a wont to use her feminine arts and allurements to accomplish her means. Why should one be deemed any more decent than the other? They were sisters, after all, Lady Catherine considered.

As if incapable of doing anything that did not render her the center of attention, young Lydia told everyone who would listen of her life in Newcastle as a married woman. How dreary it was compared to Brighton, she lamented. Why even Meryton bustled with excitement by comparison, she opined. Turning to her eldest sister, she said, "I understand the militia is once again settled outside of town."

Before Jane could respond, Kitty cried, "Indeed. I dare say many of the officers are every bit as handsome as your Wickham."

Elizabeth threw a cursory glance first at Georgiana and then Miss Caroline Bingley at the mention of her *brother's* name. The grimace that graced the face of the latter might have bothered Elizabeth exceedingly were this a few years ago. Now it was all she could do not to don the same expression at the mention of that man's name. Georgiana's face, on the other hand, was completely unreadable.

"La!" Lydia exclaimed. "I dare say you are insane to utter such a silly thing, Kitty, for there is not another man on Earth who is as handsome as my Wickham. I do declare he is the best man in the world."

Now it was Elizabeth's turn to look at her husband. *Will he storm out the room again in the wake of Lydia's silliness?*

Darcy, it seemed, was doing a fine imitation of a man engrossed in his book. As if oblivious of Lydia's speech, he simply turned the page.

Miss Bingley must have observed his lack of concern as well. This appalling behavior of Mrs. Bennet and her youngest daughter came as no surprise to Miss Caroline Bingley. A fine young woman with an air of decided fashion, she had seen it all before. She threw a reflective glance over the whole of her acquaintance with the Bennets, starting with those early days at Netherfield Park. At that time, Mr. Darcy knew what he was about. He abhorred the Bennets as much as she did as a consequence of their low country manners, their lack of fortune, and their want of connections.

She plainly recalled his dismal view of the Bennet daughters' marital prospects.

"If they had uncles enough to fill all of Cheapside it would not make them one jot less agreeable," her brother Charles had opined.

"But it must very materially lessen their chance of marrying men of any consideration in the world," Darcy had replied—a sentiment to which everyone save Charles gave hearty assent, and they went on to indulge their mirth for some time at the expense of Miss Jane Bennet's vulgar relations.

Her mind then flew to the time when they first knew Eliza and how amazed they were to find that she was a reputed beauty. She particularly recollected Mr. Darcy saying one night, after they had been dining at Netherfield, *"She a beauty!—I should as soon call her mother a wit,"* in reference to the woman he now called his dear wife.

How is it that, despite Mr. Darcy's former low opinion of Eliza Bennet, she now finds herself the mistress of all this when everyone knows it should have been me?

Caroline knew better than to do anything to garner Darcy's disapprobation now that he was married to Eliza Bennet, and the occasions of their being together had become few and far between. However, she did miss their verbal repartee and the manner in which they often flirted with each other before he completely surrendered his better judgement to a pair of fine eyes.

Before Eliza Bennet came along, I was certain that Mr. Darcy enjoyed our teasing banter exceedingly well—far more than he had enjoyed such intercourse with any other woman of his acquaintance. Even if he did sometimes like to pretend he was unaffected, I knew better.

Wanting to recapture even a hint of their former intimate camaraderie, she said, "No doubt it is a great comfort to all the single young ladies in want of husbands knowing the militia is back in town."

Rather than eliciting a reaction from Mr. Darcy, it was Mrs. Bennet whose sentiments were perturbed. She pursed her lips. "You must be comforted as well, Miss Bingley, for you are not getting any younger, are you? If you do not seize upon a husband soon, you may well miss your chance."

Poor Miss Bingley, Elizabeth considered, recalling how little the younger woman cared for her mama. *How little satisfaction she must now suffer in having forced my mother to say that which gave no one any pain but Miss Bingley herself.*

How relieved Miss Bingley must have felt when the two youngest Bennet daughters resumed their debate on whether there was another man whose beauty compared to Mr. Wickham's. Why, even Mrs. Bennet insisted upon having her share of the conversation. "I remember the time when I liked a red coat myself very well. Indeed, so I do still at my heart," she waxed poetically. "I dare say he was every bit as handsome as Wickham."

In the meantime, Lady Catherine took it all in. What a perfect unfolding of events this was, for as much as her ladyship liked to pretend she was shocked by the appalling behavior of Darcy's mother-in-law and his new sisters, in truth she was quite delighted. There was no other explanation for her bringing Mr. William Collins, her vicar, with her to Pemberley during a time when its new mistress was expected to shine. She meant to embarrass the new Mrs. Darcy by putting her ridiculous cousin on display for all of Derbyshire society to see.

What a stroke of luck for her that this need not be a solo act. No, among Elizabeth's mother, her younger sisters, and her cousin there would be entertainment enough to last the entire stay. Mr. Bennet Lady Catherine excused from all this. It was not that she held such a high opinion of the gentleman who had allowed his youngest daughter to run off with a man twice her age and live in sin, and who then attempted to patch up the affair at great expense to himself and his brother, so far as her ladyship knew. It was because she had only seen him for the briefest of time before he scampered off to the seclusion of Pemberley's library.

A proud woman, Lady Catherine did not easily countenance ridiculousness. Her haughty air did not dissuade Mrs. Bennet. A woman of little understanding, the latter said, "What a fine thing it is that you came all this way to take part in the festivities here at Pemberley, your ladyship."

Her ladyship reared back her head as if taking umbrage that Mrs. Bennet had spoken to her in such terms of familiarity—almost as though she felt herself Lady Catherine's equal. It did not sit well with her at all that she was forced to associate with people so heavily connected in trade. It was one thing to take part in an occasional business venture from time to time, especially when there was money to be made with so little effort on one's part. However, the idea of manual labor for the sake of maintaining one's existence on this earth was, to Lady Catherine's way of thinking, abhorrent. Either one was distinguished by rank and privilege, or one was not. To Lady Catherine, there was no in between.

Those Bingleys with whom her nephew chose to associate posed quite the conundrum for her ladyship. They were far enough away from those physical aspects of being in trade; however, as their wealth was earned in trade, they were not quite acceptable as proper members of the privileged class to warrant her ladyship's approbation. Such musings caused Lady Catherine to forget she had been spoken to. She heard the other woman clear her throat. This was sufficient to interrupt her musings but not enough to warrant any sort of response.

Mrs. Bennet tried again. "Pray you will forgive me for not begging you to take some refreshment after your walk with my Lizzy when you visited Longbourn. You went away before I had the chance."

"I assure you that would have been quite unnecessary, madam. My being there did not lend itself to such hospitality, for it was hardly a social call."

"Why, I am sorry to hear that, for I told all my neighbors that I had the honor of receiving you. Well, I suppose you will surely call on me when you are next in Hertfordshire."

"That, I assure you, is most unlikely."

"Do you mean to say you have no intention of delivering word from Mr. and Mrs. Collins the next time you find yourself in the area?"

"I most certainly will not take such a burden upon myself. Mr. Collins—your cousin— is my servant. I am not his! And I am not in the business of delivering messages."

Mrs. Bennet's face took on a puzzled expression. She looked at her second eldest daughter and back at her ladyship. "Oh, but Lizzy and I were sure that was the purpose in your calling on us at Longbourn." She gazed at her daughter. "Were we not, Lizzy?"

The last thing Elizabeth cared to think about was that fateful day. Lady Catherine's intentions in descending upon Longbourn had been abominable. She meant to guarantee that a union between her favorite nephew and Elizabeth would never happen. This brought to Elizabeth's busy mind the question of her ladyship even being at Pemberley.

I rather supposed the grand lady had severed all ties with my husband and me. This was not the time to redress old wounds. Wanting to change the subject, Elizabeth said, "Mr. Collins, how is our dear Charlotte?"

The tall, heavy-looking young man, whose air was grave and stately and whose manners were very formal, was standing by the fireplace with Mr. Gardiner and Bingley. He cleared his throat. "Mrs. Collins is in Hertfordshire. Indeed, she is spending this time away from her responsibilities in Hunsford with her family. She sends her apologies for not being here. However, I contend it is better this way. You see, my dear wife is perfectly comfortable in her station in life and, despite being a frequent guest in the home of my noble patroness, she is not so comfortable in the presence of nobility as am I."

Elizabeth was more than happy when the end of the evening spared her further company with her ladyship. Lady Catherine detested Elizabeth as much now as ever before, it seemed, and Elizabeth might easily say the same of her sentiments toward her ladyship. Her feelings had not, however, kept her from attempting to heal the breach in Darcy's relationship with his aunt as a consequence of Elizabeth and Darcy's marriage. By Elizabeth's persuasion, Darcy was prevailed upon to overlook the offense, and seek reconciliation. It had been in vain. Elizabeth's earlier attempts at reconciliation aside, she firmly believed that Darcy must bear some culpability for his aunt's behavior, just as he had expected of her where her relations were concerned. Later that evening, when Elizabeth and Darcy were preparing for bedtime, she told him as much.

"I believe you owe me an apology, sir," Elizabeth said to her husband.

"An apology? Whatever for, my love?"

"Well—as I recall, you said the other night was the worst night ever with the strongest indication that my mother and sister were to blame. I contend that that night was nothing in comparison to this evening."

"I take it you are referring to my aunt's behavior. You must understand that she likes to make her opinion known. I have grown rather accustomed to it by now."

"Is that your way of saying your aunt's ridiculousness is somehow more tolerable than my mother's? Why does that not surprise me?"

"It doesn't surprise you because it shouldn't surprise you."

"What does surprise me, sir, is the level of your hypocrisy."

"I do not make the rules, my love."

"And what rule would that be? What is considered as ridiculousness in those you deem beneath your sphere is somehow estimable in those in the aristocracy?"

"Exactly. Is there any wonder I love you so much? Not only are you the most charming, the wittiest, and the handsomest woman of my acquaintance, but you are also a fast learner."

"Oh, Mr. Darcy! If it were not for our ridiculous rule of never going to bed angry, you would surely find yourself in my bad graces for such a remark—rather insult layered in sweetness."

"Yes, and you knew this about me, yet you fell in love with me still. You knew that I would never truly bear the ridiculousness of others and that is why you gave yourself so much trouble of shielding me from your aunt Mrs. Philips as well as several others during the days of our courtship. Do not suppose for one second that I was unaware of what you were doing or that I did not love you even more for your compassion."

"First of all, you mean you would not truly bear the ridiculousness of anyone other than Lady Catherine."

"Yes, that is precisely what I mean. Even you will allow that, despite my aunt's eccentricities, there is no denying her benevolence. She is greatly esteemed by those in our circle."

"I find it interesting, sir, that you consider her ladyship as anything resembling benevolent. I consider her manner a mixture of condescension and unmasked disdain."

"No, I am rather certain the disdain did not manifest itself until after she had suspected you and I were engaged." His spirits rising to playfulness even at Elizabeth's expense, he said, "Let us not forget all the good fortune her actions inadvertently brought into our lives."

"And this must be your excuse for her!" She threw up her hands. "You are unbelievable, Mr. Darcy!"

"You're unbelievable, Mrs. Darcy. Have you forgotten all the warmth and kindness she extended to you when you were in Kent? Your relations, as a whole, are quite in arrears in terms of extending that same level of generosity to me."

"Does your uncharitable assessment extend to Uncle and Aunt Gardiner, sir?"

"Oh, no—forgive me. The Gardiners' generosity I must exclude from my grievances."

"It is comforting to know that you find at least two of my relations unobjectionable. However, I believe I did Uncle and Aunt Philips a great disservice in limiting their time in your company and you in theirs. Perhaps I ought to make amends by writing to invite them to join as at Pemberley as well. Nearly everyone else from our families has descended upon us. It seems terribly unfair that they should be excluded. Why should they not have their share of the fun?" Elizabeth asked in a voice similar to Lydia's.

Dread overspread Darcy's countenance. "You would not dare."

"Do not tempt me, sir. What's more, I shall send one of the Darcy carriages to bring them here. Just imagine all the refinement and culture that might wear off on them during their travels, and they shall stay at all the finest establishments that you patronize as well. I am excited just thinking about the scheme."

"Pray do not give yourself the trouble, I beseech you. Our party is quite large enough as it is."

"I will forego my plan on one condition, sir."

"Pray what condition is that? I will agree to anything."

"You must desist in your hypocrisy and show my family the same amount of deference and tolerance as you show your own family."

Darcy exhaled. "Is that all?"

"You seem rather too relieved. What exactly did you expect me to say?"

"Well—for a moment I thought you were going to tell me that George Wickham should be allowed to attend the dinner party. You and I both know it is Lydia's favorite wish."

"Sir, nothing you can ever do or say would warrant punishment as severe as that, I assure you."

Chapter 6

His Solemn Duty

The evening of Elizabeth's dinner party finally had arrived. Everyone who was anyone in the county was assembled in Pemberley's dining room. It was Elizabeth's moment to shine—to impress upon those who questioned Darcy's decision to eschew society's expectations as well as his family's by choosing a wife from outside his sphere.

Elegantly adorned women and handsomely attired gentleman sat at the host of tables appropriately arranged to accommodate the rather large gathering. At what would be the head sat Darcy himself. Elizabeth sat at his right, Georgiana his left. Beyond them sat Lord and Lady Fitzwilliam, The Earl and Countess of Matlock, Lady Catherine de Bourgh and her daughter Miss Anne de Bourgh, Mr. and Mrs. Charles Bingley, Miss Caroline Bingley, Mr. and Mrs. Gardiner, Mr. William Collins, Mr. and Mrs. Bennet, Miss Mary Bennet, and Miss Kitty Bennet.

Deliberately interspersed between the Darcys' relations were many of the wealthiest personages in Derbyshire and parts of the neighboring counties. Conspicuously absent was Mrs. Lydia Wickham. Elizabeth did not know whether to rejoice in her good fortune or worry that some ill fate had befallen her sister who had spent the best part of the day in Lambton with her dear husband. She settled upon the latter. Sensing her increasing concern, Darcy had taken Elizabeth by the hand just before the first course. "If something has happened," he said in a low voice, "we would have heard about it. You must not make yourself uneasy. Trust me, all is well."

The luster of fine china, the sparkling glitter of exquisite crystal glasses, and the warm glow of the host of candelabras all about the room spoke not only of Darcy's wealth but to the elegance of the occasion. At length, the soft buzz of genteel conversation, the gentle clatter of sterling silver eating utensils, and the occasionally raised glasses in a toast to the mistress of Pemberley conspired to make Elizabeth forget that her youngest sister had forfeited her part in the evening's gaiety.

Things took a decided turn when the third course was being served and in waltzed Elizabeth's wayward sister. As though realizing how late she was, Lydia placed her fingers on her mouth. "La! I am ever so sorry for my tardiness, but I could hardly tear myself away from my dear Wickham, who so wanted to be here himself."

Elizabeth felt the color spread all over her body. Remembering herself, she looked at the butler. "Pray prepare a place for my sister."

Mrs. Althea Grantham, who resided at the neighboring estate and whose husband had more than six thousand pounds a year, said, "Pardon me, young woman. Did you say your husband's name is Wickham?" Speaking to no one in particular, she continued, "What an uncanny coincidence this is. If I recall correctly, the late Mr. Darcy's steward was named Wickham."

"Coincidence? I think not. The late Mr. Darcy was my Wickham's godfather. In fact, my dear Wickham was always Mr. Darcy's favorite, though one would never know it. Did you know that my Wickham is not allowed to set foot at Pemberley?" She looked at her sister pointedly. "Is that not true, Lizzy?"

"No doubt you regale in discussing your husband; however, I pray you will give us all leave to enjoy this evening by avoiding those matters best discussed in privacy."

"I agree, wholeheartedly, with Mrs. Darcy," said Lord Edward Fitzwilliam, Darcy's uncle, who prided himself not only because he was a peer, but because he was the head of the noble Fitzwilliam family.

Lydia said, "La! I do not know what all this fuss is about. My Wickham is the best man I know. Even you dare not argue with me, Lizzy. The whole world knows he was your favorite for the longest time." She turned to her mother. "Isn't that true, Mama?"

Normally eager for her share in the conversation, Lydia's words rendered Mrs. Bennet speechless.

This was insufficient inducement for young Lydia to hold her tongue. "Many a young woman would love to trade places with me. Am I not correct, Georgiana?" Lydia took a sip of wine in an attempt to mask a knowing simper. "From what my Wickham has told me, Georgiana might have been the one in my place, only she is not as clever as I am."

Heads lurched, jerked, twisted, and turned with Lydia's pronouncement, not that she took any notice of the turmoil overtaking the room. Lydia said, "You should see the way they stop and stare whenever my Wickham and I enter a room. He is the most handsome, the most charming man in the world."

Elizabeth was appalled. That wicked man had indeed told his silly wife things she did not need to know, and soon everyone in the room would be privy to the Ramsgate affair if she did not do something. She looked at her father, pleadingly, to entreat his interference.

Taking the hint, Mr. Bennet, an odd mixture of quick parts, sarcastic humor, reserve, and caprice, picked up his napkin and wiped his mouth. Standing, he said, "Lydia, my dear, I know this is rather untoward, but I really am in need of a word with you."

"Oh, Papa! Can it not wait? I only just arrived, and I am famished. My Wickham and I had no time to eat as a consequence of our being forced to spend so many of our nights apart from each other."

"Come along, my dear," said he, assisting his daughter to her feet.

All the pride and joy that Mr. Bennet felt over the marriages of his two eldest daughters to two honorable and, yes, wealthy young men was nothing in comparison to the shame he now suffered as a result of Lydia's inexcusable behavior that evening.

This is my fault, he silently berated himself. Certainly, years of over-indulgence and adoration by a mother of mean understanding, little information, and uncertain temper played a large part in how Lydia turned out, but years of neglect and disparagement by a father was the greater factor. A reflective glance over the entirety of his youngest daughter's life gave him cause to consider that she wanted nothing but attention. With four older children and not one of them a male child to carry on his name and inherit his estate, Mr. Bennet simply had no such attention to give.

What had he done during those times when Lydia needed a father's guidance as well as a father's hand but laughed at her? What had he done when she needed a father's presence as well as a father's supervision but stolen away to the solace of his library? And what had he done when the daughter whom he boasted aloud of being his favorite warned him that no good would come from his indifference toward allowing young Lydia to go away to Brighton that fateful summer but made sport of her concern?

"Do not make yourself uneasy, my love," he had said upon seeing that Elizabeth's whole heart was in the subject. *"We shall have no peace at Longbourn if Lydia does not go to Brighton. Let her go then. Colonel Forster is a sensible man. He will keep her out of any real mischief. She is luckily too poor to be an object of prey to anybody. At Brighton, she will be of less importance even as a common flirt than she has been here. The officers will find women better worth their notice. Let us hope, therefore, that her being there may teach her of her own insignificance. At any rate, she cannot grow many degrees worse, without authorizing us to lock her up for the rest of her life."*

He shook his head in remembrance of ever having uttered those words. *I have no one to blame but myself.*

"Papa," Lydia cried, thus interrupting his silent self-recriminations, "why did you insist on speaking to me in private? Could whatever it is that you wish to say to me not wait for Heaven's sake? I hardly had a bite to eat all day, for I fully intended to make up for my lapse at dinner and now what am I to do?"

"Perhaps if you had spent more time eating and less time attempting to make yourself ridiculous in front of your sister's guests, there would have been no need for my intervention."

"La! I was merely doing my best to add a bit of liveliness where there was none." With a self-satisfied smile, she said, "Lizzy and her haughty old husband ought to be thanking me."

"Have you ever once considered that it is you who ought to be thanking the two of them?"

Her mouth gaped. "Why would I thank the two of them when they have so much and my Wickham and I have so very little? Those two deserve no such gratitude from me. Darcy especially does not, for his selfishness is what led to my husband's diminished circumstances. My Wickham reminded me of as much when he and I were together earlier." She shuddered in feigned disgust. "Oh! Papa, it was so very dreadful to have to spend the better part of the day in that drab little room in the inn at Lambton. I hope Lizzy and Darcy are pleased with themselves for forcing my Wickham and me to endure such dreadful conditions."

"Lydia! Even you cannot be so foolish as to fail to realize that Darcy's benevolence is the reason you are not living on the streets of London. You cannot be unaware that he would not rest until he found you, and that he practically forced Wickham to marry you to spare you a life of disgrace. He saved our entire family's reputation and at considerable cost to himself, I must concede. He paid the bulk of your husband's debts. He paid for your husband's commission in Newcastle. The entire expense was upwards of ten thousand pounds, and this is how you repay him."

"Found me!" Lydia exclaimed with excitement. "How do you suppose he found me when I was never lost? I was safe and secure with my dear Wickham the entire time. As for practically forcing my husband to marry me, that is nothing more than a deliberate falsehood. My Wickham could hardly wait to marry me. He promised me he would make me the happiest woman in the world every single day and night. How dare Darcy try to take credit for that! Although none of this ought to come as a surprise to me. My Wickham tells me time and again how much Darcy likes to have his own way."

Mr. Bennet said, "Pray what explanation did your Wickham provide for the ten thousand pounds Darcy spent to patch-up your husband's debauched affairs?"

"I posit ten thousand pounds is merely a pittance to what Darcy can afford, and, what's more, I am sure he would not have parted with a single shilling if not for his ill-treatment of my Wickham for the better part of his life. As well informed as you are, Papa, you surely must know that Darcy denied my dear Wickham the living in Kympton that ought to have been his."

Mr. Bennet threw up his hands. There was no amending his failures in regards to Lydia, and he did not mean to spend another minute of his time attempting to do so. *I have done my part, at least for this one night, by removing her from polite society. I have neither the inclination nor the patience to do more.* Thus resolved, he walked to the door and, without looking back, he quit the room. *Reining in Lydia is no longer my concern. She has a husband for that.*

He did, however, remain close by outside the door to assure that Lydia stayed put for the duration of the meal. Later, when he observed the women making their way to the parlor, he decided to abandon his post and join the gentlemen for port.

Not only did he need a drink, but he also needed a good measure of sensible conversation to wash away the memory of the time spent earlier alone with Lydia.

The first person he saw upon entering the increasingly smoke-filled room was his cousin, Mr. Collins. Lydia's foolishness was nothing in comparison to what Mr. Bennet might encounter in that quarter. Congratulating himself that William Collins was one man he did not have to call his son-in-law, the elderly man went directly to the opposite end of the room. At least he could take credit for having done something right by not siding with his wife when she insisted that their second eldest daughter accept the foolish man's hand in marriage. *Oh, what a grave mistake that would have been,* he considered with a swift shake of his head.

As a man of the cloth, Mr. William Collins thought it was his solemn duty to distance himself from the Bennets and to abdicate himself of the appalling behavior of the youngest Bennet daughter in the eyes of all those gathered there who would one day be his peers.

He walked up to a Mr. Harry Rollins, whose estate abutted Pemberley. Clearing his throat, the proud man said, "Mr. William Collins at your service, sir."

The older gentleman's blank stare compelled Mr. Collins to continue. "You will recall my having greeted you earlier. I am Mrs. Darcy's cousin and the heir apparent to her father's estate—Longbourn in Hertfordshire."

A portly man with an air of importance about him, the gentleman raised his glass. "I offer a toast to Mr. Bennet's health. May he live long and prosper."

"Indeed, may he live long and prosper." Mr. Collins cleared his throat again. "Sir, I wanted to take the liberty of apologizing to you on my cousin's behalf for the appalling spectacle at dinner. As you have likely

P. O. DIXON

discerned, Mrs. Darcy is a paragon of virtue by comparison. Although there was a time when I too found myself questioning her judgment, I want to assure you that her character is beyond reproach. She is not to be judged by her sister's behavior."

"Ah, you need not worry on that account, Mr. Collins. We all have members of our families who ought not to be exposed to polite society, do we not? Although, in Mrs. Wickham's case, I must say she is quite refreshing. Her husband is indeed a most fortunate man."

"Sir, if you knew the circumstances of that union then you would not be nearly so charitable in your good opinion. The fact is that the alliance came about as the consequence of a scandalous elopement that threatened to ruin the entire family's reputation.

"In view of my situation in life and by my relationship with Mrs. Darcy's excellent father, I condoled with him on the grievous affliction he had suffered. It was beyond my power to say or do anything that would alleviate so severe a misfortune. I posited that the death of his daughter would have been a blessing by comparison."

Here, the other man retrieved his pocket watch and gave it a determined stare. This was insufficient to discourage Collins's speech and thus he continued.

"In relating the particulars of the affair to my noble patroness, Lady Catherine de Bourgh, she aptly pointed out that no one would wish to connect themselves with such a family. Indeed, this led me to consider that, if a certain event of a certain November had unfolded otherwise, I would have been directly involved in the sorrow and disgrace. I cannot tell you how disappointed I was when Mr. Bennet disregarded my advice to throw off the unworthy young lady from his affections forever and leave her to reap the fruits of her heinous offence."

Twisting his strained neck, Collins swallowed hard. "I say all this not to be a party to gossip, but merely to beg your forgiveness and disabuse you of any notion that Mrs. Wickham's indecorous deportment is a reflection of her excellent sister's good character."

"Mrs. Darcy is fortunate to have a cousin who goes to such lengths to protect her good name. I assure you that I was not the least bit offended by the events of the evening. Now, if you will pardon me, I think the time is near for us to join the ladies."

Collins, feeling quite pleased to have done his cousin such a benevolent service, was encouraged by his reception. Still, there were some matters that he supposed might have been more aptly conveyed. After pausing a moment or two to refashion his speech, he spotted another of Darcy's neighbors standing by the mantelpiece observing the goings-on. Ever cognizant of his duty to his cousin Elizabeth, Collins gave his coat a sharp tug and then set off in the gentleman's direction.

~~~

Lady Catherine silently applauded the unseemly spectacle that took place over dinner earlier that evening. Mr. Collins was a paragon of good taste and proper breeding in comparison to that wild Bennet daughter. If she had but one regret it was that Mr. Bennet had taken it upon himself to spare the rest of the Darcys' guests from his silly daughter's company when he did. Still, she had said enough to pique her ladyship's curiosity exceedingly.

Glancing about the room, her ladyship's eyes landed on the one person who was both knowledgeable of what Mrs. Wickham was talking about and willing to fill in the details of all that had gone unspoken.

Lady Catherine stole the empty seat beside Miss Caroline Bingley. Eschewing many of the usual pleasantries, her ladyship came directly to the point. "I understand you were in Hertfordshire yourself when my nephew suffered the misfortune of making the Bennet family's acquaintance." Lady Catherine's tone was meant to be intimate to disguise the fact that she did not particularly care for the young woman whose company she must endure in order to accomplish her purposes.

Fashionably attired in a rich, auburn satin gown, Caroline discreetly scanned the room to see who was close by. Whatever were her private thoughts on the matter at hand, she was not eager to disparage Elizabeth aloud. Pemberley may not have been her home, nor would it possibly ever be, but she really did enjoy being there. On the other hand, the temptation to earn her ladyship's approbation was strong. Old habits did not die easily.

"Indeed, I was there to witness it all. Although, I never truly supposed then that the likes of those Bennets would one day roam the halls of Pemberley."

"My nephew was determined to have Elizabeth, and thus he must live with this choice. What I am curious to know is this." Her ladyship leaned closer. "Is there any truth to what that appalling young woman had to say during dinner? Did Elizabeth indeed esteem George Wickham? Was he truly her favorite? Did the two of them have an understanding?"

"I can say that every word of what Mrs. Wickham said is true. Eliza's head was full of the dashing lieutenant, and she did not tolerate anyone who dared to discredit him—especially Mr. Darcy. I ought to know for on more than one occasion I witnessed the two of them in a heated debate over that gentleman. I even tried to warn her of her folly for admiring the son of the late Mr. Darcy's steward as well. She practically laughed in my face."

Lady Catherine held up her hand signaling that she had heard enough. A new resolve glossed over her ladyship's countenance. She always believed there was a flaw in Elizabeth's character that would prove her unworthy of the trust her nephew had placed in her to be the mistress of his home and one day the mother of his yet unborn children. *The sister of my only niece!* Finally, Lady Catherine knew exactly how to act.

To Elizabeth and Darcy's dismay, Lydia made her way back to the party later that evening and soon captured the attention of every gentleman in the room who was known for having wandering eyes, much to Lydia's satisfaction and the dismay of the gentlemen's wives.

Despite all the attention she had garnered, it seemed Lydia was determined to embarrass her sister even more, and she prevailed upon Mary to open the instrument and play. Bored as could be, and always impatient for display, Mary readily acceded to her sister's plea for a lively tune to add a bit of gaiety to a room that the latter insisted was severely wanting. This was meant to be a party, she contended—not a wake. The only thing left for Lydia to do was to prevail on the others to rally to her cause. Kitty quickly joined in her sister's campaign and soon the youngest Bennet daughters and their willing partners, as well as two or three other young couples, commenced dancing at one end of the room.

Several of the other guests stood near them in silent indignation at such a mode of passing the evening at the expense of pleasant conversation. If the Darcys had meant for this to be a ball then they should have indeed given a ball, some of the older, rather patrician women could be heard remarking among themselves.

Darcy himself was also dismayed. He likened what was unfolding before his eyes to what had occurred on that evening at Lucas Lodge in Hertfordshire. That had been during the earlier days of his acquaintance with the people of Meryton. He had equated the appalling display to savagery. He never imagined he would one day bear witness to such an exhibition in his own home.

Lydia soon prevailed upon a Mr. John Turner, from a nearby estate, who was rumored to be a rake of the truest kind despite his being on the wrong side of forty, to dance with her. Not long after that, the two of them drifted to a corner of the room where no one could be bothered by either of them, other than the gentleman's wife. Not one to be thus disrespected, the injured woman marched across the room and inserted herself directly between her husband and Lydia. Her own reputation attested to the fact that she did not garner the attention of the rakish John Turner by being demure and unassuming. Lydia Wickham may well have cast herself as fodder for derision because of her outrageous behavior that evening, but not at Mrs. Sally Turner's expense.

Laughing at the ridiculousness of others was part of Elizabeth's nature, but not that night—not when the others in question were members of her own family. Standing alone on the terrace, she exhaled deeply. Gazing up at the nighttime's sky in wonder, she watched as the moon ducked behind the clouds. What a balm the fresh, crisp air was for her mortified nerves. Memories of another night a couple years past came to mind: the night of the Netherfield ball. She was certain she would never forget her family's appalling behavior that evening, even if she lived to be a hundred years old. Now history was repeating itself with Mary's mediocre performance on the pianoforte, her mother's excessive boasting about her eldest daughters' good fortunes, her cousin Mr. Collins's sycophancy, and Lydia's wildness.

Will my family ever forego a chance to make themselves ridiculous? Elizabeth threw a reflective glance over the events of the evening. *Thank heavens Papa heeded my silent plea to escort Lydia away from the formal dining room.* She pursed her lips. *If only he might have prevented her from returning afterward.* Her mind wandered to the one person in the room who must certainly have taken a perverted pleasure in the goings-on: Lady Catherine de Bourgh. The haughty aristocrat's words echoed in Elizabeth's busy mind.

Are the shades of Pemberley to be thus polluted?

Such had been her complaint when confronting Elizabeth at Longbourn that fateful day. *Indeed, her ladyship must be thoroughly pleased.* It had not escaped Elizabeth's notice that Lady Catherine and Miss Caroline Bingley were embroiled in a private tête-à-tête earlier that evening as well. *No doubt both of them are pleased.*

Just as the moon emerged from behind the clouds, Elizabeth tore her eyes away from the sky and espied her husband walking her way. When they were close, he reached both hands out to her, and she readily accepted them. At that moment, his tender touch was exactly what she needed.

"My family," she began, her voice filled with apology. "How can I make amends?"

Releasing her hands, he placed a finger to her slightly parted lips. "You owe me nothing, my love." He took her in his arms and drew her closer. No distance existed between them. He placed his hands along either side of her long, slender neckline, leaned in, and gently brushed a kiss over her lips. "Come back inside, my love."

Time and again, she had been a witness to her family's lack of decorum. He had seen it too, yet, instead of berating himself for willingly marrying into such a family, he was standing there offering her comfort at a time when she wanted it the most. Elizabeth truly loved this man. Her forehead against his, her hands rested on his waist. Comforted beyond measure by his nearness, she spoke softly. "Must we?"

He lifted her chin and kissed her. "We must."

Darcy was not immune to his wife's sentiments. He would rather the evening were over as well. He was ever so thankful that his sister was not there to witness the evening's unfolding events. Although she was not officially out in Society, Darcy and Elizabeth saw no harm in her taking part in the evening's events. Georgiana had complained of a headache soon after dinner and retired to her apartment. If only he could spare Elizabeth. She had worked so hard to make the evening a success.

She had even salvaged what was left of the dinner after Lydia had been ushered away by her father. Such was not an easy feat, but Elizabeth's charming manner won out and without making excuses for her sister. Her loyalty to her family was beyond question, but she certainly deserved an equal measure from them. To Darcy's way of thinking, she was not getting any such consideration.

Heedless of decorum and his obligation to entertain the guests, he stayed by Elizabeth's side for the remainder of the evening until the last of their visitors who were not staying overnight took their leave. The happenings of that evening gave him much to consider. The matter of houseguests running amok was certainly something Darcy had never planned on. Family loyalty had its limits, and so far as he was concerned those limits had been grossly exceeded.

Chapter 7

Ought to Know

The next day, the Earl of Matlock walked into his nephew's study. "Darcy, I wanted to wait until your guests had left before I spoke with you."

This visit from his uncle was not wholly unexpected. It was patently clear that his lordship had been appalled by the events of the previous evening. However, if he expected an apology, he had come to the wrong place.

Standing, Darcy said, "My lord—"

The earl held up his hand. "Hear what I have to say, Nephew. You have long prided yourself on being your own master. You follow your own counsel. I would expect no less from you. However, I am the head of this family. If there are events that have unfolded that would prove to damage our family's reputation were they widely discovered then I ought to know about them."

"What is it that you think I have been keeping from you, Uncle?"

"What is the meaning of Mrs. Wickham's outlandish assertion that Georgiana might have been in her place? Is there something about my niece that you have been keeping from me?"

Disguise of any sort was Darcy's abhorrence. Though he and Richard had taken great pains to assure that Georgiana's secret remained concealed, now that Lydia had hinted of having knowledge of the Ramsgate affair there was no point in denying it to the titular head of the family.

Darcy took a seat and his uncle did likewise. "You are aware," the younger man began, "that my sister had long retained a favorable impression of George Wickham's kindness to her as a child."

"So this does have something to do with Wickham!"

"Indeed. I have always known about his vile propensities, but I never shared my knowledge with my sister." Darcy went on to explain how Wickham had followed Georgiana to Ramsgate a while ago and had persuaded her to consent to an elopement.

The color drained from the earl's face. Before he could fashion a protest, Darcy said, "Matters did not progress that far." He went on to explain how he had arrived in Ramsgate in time to save his sister from a horrendous mistake. "I am happy to add that I owed the knowledge of the entire sordid affair to my sister herself. I joined them unexpectedly a day or two before the intended elopement, and then Georgiana, unable to support the idea of grieving and offending me and possibly wishing I might sanction the would-be alliance, acknowledged the whole of it to me. You may imagine what I felt and how I acted. Regard for my sister's credit and feelings prevented any public exposure. I wrote to Wickham, who left the place immediately, and I removed Mrs. Younge from her charge. Wickham's chief object was unquestionably my sister's fortune, but I cannot help supposing that the hope of revenging himself on me was a strong inducement, as well. His revenge would have been complete indeed."

"You kept all of this from me!" the earl exclaimed. "Did you not consider that this is the sort of thing I need to know given my standing in the community—amongst the *ton*?" His breathing a bit shallower than usual, the earl rested his hand on his chest. "Who else knows of this? Does my son Richard know?"

Colonel Richard Fitzwilliam walked into the room. Having arrived at Pemberley during the wee hours of the morning, he had missed out entirely on all the prior evening's excitement. "Do I know what?" he asked, throwing himself into the closest chair.

"Darcy has finally seen fit to enlighten me on what occurred in Ramsgate. Did you know Georgiana was nearly tempted to engage in a scandalous elopement with the son of her father's steward? Of course you did! Who else knows?" He looked at Darcy pointedly.

"Does your wife know? Is she the one who shared this information with her silly sister?"

"Yes, my wife knows, and, no, she most certainly did not tell Mrs. Wickham. How dare you accuse her of such an indelicacy?"

"How could you have told Elizabeth and not me or Lady Ellen, for that matter? Is my wife not charged with bringing Georgiana out next Season? Surely you did not suppose Elizabeth capable of bringing out the niece of the Earl of Matlock and presenting her at court."

"Now you dare to question my wife's ability?"

"I question no one's capabilities! Did you ask Lady Ellen to oversee Georgiana's coming out as a means of thwarting Lady Catherine, or did you not? Just as it was my sister Anne's fondest wish that you should marry young Anne, it was also her favorite wish that our sister Catherine play a part in arranging Georgiana's coming out. I did you a great favor by siding against Catherine as you requested. I shall not be a party to disappointing my own wife."

"I am rather certain that Lady Ellen and Elizabeth shall devise a means of sharing the responsibilities inherent in my sister's first Season."

At that moment, Lady Catherine, who, unbeknownst to the others, had been listening outside the door, stormed into the room. "That is where you are mistaken, Nephew. I have always questioned the wisdom of your knowingly marrying the sister of a woman who was foolish enough to run off with George Wickham. After what I learned just last evening that

Elizabeth herself was once a great admirer of that despicable man—that he was a favorite of hers long before he ran off with her youngest sister, did you think I would not know how to act? Do you suppose for one moment that I will allow her to have a say in my niece's coming out and her presentation at court? You give me no choice other than to remove Georgiana from Pemberley altogether.

"My sister must certainly be turning over in her grave knowing the type of people to whom you have exposed her precious daughter. It will take all the upcoming months under my stewardship to remove the corrupting influence those Bennets have had on my niece, and to remind her who she is and what is expected of her during her coming out season. I demand that you surrender Georgiana to my care immediately, else I shall seek legal remedy. Do not suppose for one instance that it is beyond my power."

"Catherine!" Lord Matlock shouted.

She glared at her brother. "What have I said that is untrue? You saw it all, and I know you well enough to know you were just as appalled as I was by all that occurred last evening. How might Elizabeth possibly be expected to protect or to serve as an example for Georgiana when she failed to protect her own sister? Worse still, she might just as easily have fallen prey to Wickham's trap herself. I am convinced she merely lacked opportunity."

"It is true that Elizabeth herself may have made mistakes in judgment, but she is Darcy's wife, and she is not to be disparaged." Lord Matlock turned to his nephew. "I know not how you should go about it, but surely you comprehend the need to put greater distance between your lovely wife and her abominable family."

His own master since the age of four and twenty, Darcy was not in the habit of following the edicts of others. He did not intend to start that morning. "No disrespect intended, but neither of you has any say in the matter. I am my sister's legal guardian, as is Richard. What is more, the timing of her coming out is for the two of us to decide."

An amiable fellow, whose opinions seldom strayed from his younger cousin's, the colonel made an attempt at rallying to Darcy's cause. "Here, here," he asserted.

After giving her nephew a look that brooked no further interruption on his part, her ladyship pierced her nephew Darcy with an equally dismissive glare. "What is there to decide? Georgiana is nearly nineteen. What in heavens are you waiting for? Pray your dear wife, who never had a proper coming out owing to her low birth, is not a factor in your decision. What are Georgiana's chances of finding a suitable match when all the other young ladies will be seventeen and eighteen? She will have her coming out this Season. My mother, my sister Anne and I were but eighteen when we celebrated our debut in society and Georgiana will be able to boast of doing likewise."

When the ordeal was finally finished, Darcy demanded that all of his noble relations leave his study. When they were gone, he pushed away from the desk and stretched himself to ease his long legs. He massaged his temple. He was not nearly as impressed with his relations now as he had been at the start of the day. The earl he could easily forgive, for Darcy knew he meant no harm but was merely expressing opinions in keeping with his noble upbringing and his place in their family's hierarchy. Toward Lady Catherine he was not so benevolent. She had gone too far.

Chapter 8

Take No Leave

Lydia barged into Elizabeth's sitting room with her mother trailing along behind her. "What is the meaning of this, Lizzy? Why is there a maid in my apartment going through my things?"

"It is time for you to take your leave of Pemberley. A carriage awaits you as soon as your belongings are packed."

Lydia crossed one arm over the other and stamped her foot. "This is all Darcy's doing. I am certain of it. He has poisoned you against your own sister—your own flesh and blood—and made you forget who you are and what you are about. Who would have thought that my own sister would become so high and mighty?"

To own the truth, Elizabeth had not breathed a word of her intentions to her husband. She had no need to involve him. She loved her sister, of that there could be no doubt. She had spent the earliest part of the dinner party worrying over Lydia's absence the evening before. Loving one's sibling was natural and did not require explanation. Allowing said sibling to take advantage of her and exhibit such callous disregard toward not only her feelings but also those of her husband, of Georgiana, and the world in general was not natural and such thoughtlessness should not be tolerated.

"Do not be ridiculous, Lydia. It is your own egregious conduct from the moment you first arrived—uninvited, I might add—that has led to this. Pray learn to accept some responsibility for the consequences of your actions. Did you truly think I would allow you to remain at Pemberley after your blatant disregard for Georgiana's feelings last evening? You came here for the sole purpose of creating havoc! Well, congratulate yourself on your success. As soon as your bags are packed you will be on your way to your *dear* husband in Lambton."

"Oh, Lizzy," Mrs. Bennet exclaimed, "why on Earth are you banishing your sister to that horrid little inn in Lambton when there is more than enough room here at Pemberley? Is it not bad enough that our dear Wickham has been forced to stay there when he ought to have been here all along with the rest of the family?"

"It's all Darcy's fault. He hates my Wickham, and he has turned Lizzy against him too. He is such a mean-spirited bully who always likes to have his own way."

"Enough, Lydia! You ought to be thankful that my husband allowed you to stay as long as you have. Besides, he knows nothing about any of this. It is my decision for you to remove yourself from my home. Would that I might have acted sooner, and then we all might have been spared the unseemly spectacle last evening."

"Oh, Lizzy, you are merely jealous that all of the gentlemen were paying attention to me and not you. Is it my fault that I am the youngest and the prettiest? Men naturally flock to me wherever I go."

Mrs. Bennet nodded. "That is true. Just as it was with me when I was her age—it is now so with my Lydia. That is no reason for you to be jealous, Lizzy, especially when you have managed to secure such a fine husband of your own."

Refusing to hold her tongue, Elizabeth said, "I intend no disrespect, Mama, but if you are so upset about Lydia's leave-taking, perhaps you ought to join her."

"Why! I shall speak to your father at once." Spinning on her heels and heading to the door, she said, "Mr. Bennet will prevail on you to change your mind about Lydia's presence at Pemberley."

~~~

After meeting with his housekeeper, Darcy sat alone in his study in deep reflection of what his uncle had to say about putting distance between Elizabeth and her Bennet relations. Supposing that he wanted to, how could he even broach such a subject with Elizabeth?

Darcy stood and walked to the window. *My wife's family means everything to her—even her sister Lydia. I remember how long it took her to accustom herself to her new life in Derbyshire, owing to its far distance from Hertfordshire and her beloved Longbourn.*

Even though Longbourn was entailed to the male line of the family, Darcy had a strong suspicion that Elizabeth would always consider it her home. Her days of youth spent there would live on in her heart and mind for eternity.

Then there was the matter of their unborn children. Surely Elizabeth would wish for her children to know their maternal relations just as he would never wish to deprive them of their paternal family.

In some ways, his children would have the same type of concerns as he faced as a child. The Fitzwilliams were as steeped in aristocracy as any of the great families in England. Their acceptance of his father and the Darcy connections that it brought would never have happened had he not been from one of the oldest and richest landed gentries in Derbyshire. It was generally known that the greatest wish of his maternal grandfather, the late Earl of Matlock, was that his daughter Lady Anne would marry a peer.

Even his aunt had married a man who was not a peer—Sir Louis de Bourgh. Then again, he was one of the richest men in Kent and had received his title as a result. An 'honorary' title combined with great fortune washed away all of the late earl's possible objections.

No doubt, if Elizabeth's father could boast of such wealth and connections, his uncle would never have suggested such a thing as he had. Darcy crossed the room and poured himself a drink. He certainly felt he needed it after the morning he'd had. He took a sip. Deeper reflection gave him to consider that it was not merely the Bennets' lack of fortune and connections that informed his uncle's speech. It was the matter of Elizabeth's roots in trade and the ensuing consequences therein, as well.

Yes, Mrs. Bennet can be vulgar, but if one were to erase the trappings of wealth that surrounded many of the people of the ton, would they be described as anything different? Such thoughts led him to ponder the way his parents' love for each other had withstood those diverse aspects of their families and specifically the manner in which his mother and father had reared him.

Painful recollections will intrude which cannot, which ought not to, be repelled. I have been a selfish being all my life, in practice, though not in principle. As a child I was taught what was right, but I was not taught to correct my temper. I was given good principles but left to follow them in pride and conceit. Unfortunately, an only son, and for many years an only child, I was spoilt by my parents. Though good themselves, they allowed, encour-

aged, almost taught me to be selfish and overbearing, to care for none beyond my own family circle, to think meanly of all the rest of the world, and to wish at least to think meanly of their sense and worth compared with my own.

Such had been his speech to Elizabeth when he had attempted to shed some light on how his upbringing had formed his opinion of others for the better part of his life. There were some lessons that one did not have to learn. He would not make the same mistakes with his children. He could not even if he wished it, for Elizabeth would never stand for it. Together they would raise their children to show compassion for others with unpretentiousness and impartiality as opposed to self-importance and bias. With prayer and good fortune, their children would be people whom both families would proudly embrace as their own.

Darcy had but one obstacle standing in his way and thus the purpose of his earlier meeting with Mrs. Reynolds. Now he only needed to brace himself for the resulting onslaught.

No sooner had he finished his thought than Colonel Fitzwilliam walked into the room. He made his way directly to Darcy's finest spirits and poured himself a drink. He silently begged his cousin to join him. Darcy declined, pointing out his own half empty snifter. His drink in hand, the colonel took a seat in his favorite chair.

"I feel I ought to apologize to you and your lovely wife for arriving too late for her party," he began. "It could not be helped. From the sound of things, I missed out on quite a lively evening."

"I would rather not discuss it," said Darcy.

"No doubt your mind is busily engaged with more recent events. Do you believe our aunt Lady Catherine will act upon her threat to seize Georgiana's guardianship?"

"She can try, but her efforts will be wasted."

"Then you are not at all concerned that she might very well prevail?"

"I am not. However, I am livid that she threatened me. It was a grave mistake on her part, and now she must live with the consequences."

"What are you planning, Cousin?"

Before Darcy could respond, Lady Catherine pushed the door of his study open and barged into the room. She said, "What on Earth is the meaning of this, Nephew? Why are my belongings being packed without my instruction? I plan to remain here at Pemberley for the rest of the week to allow my niece ample time to accustom herself to the fact that she will be leaving Pemberley and coming to live at Rosings."

"Did you think I would allow you to remain in my home after you blatantly disparaged my wife and threatened to remove Georgiana from my supervision?"

Lady Catherine picked up her bejeweled walking stick and pointed it at Darcy. "This is all Elizabeth's doing. I am certain of it. She has poisoned you against your own aunt—your own flesh and blood—and made you forget who you are and what you are about. Who would have ever thought that my own nephew could be brought so low?"

"I have heard enough, Lady Catherine! You ought to be thankful that I allowed you to remain here at Pemberley for as long as you have, especially given that you arrived—uninvited, I might add—with the sole purpose of wreaking havoc and ruining my wife's first formal dinner party. Well, congratulate yourself. Take a bow, and then be on your way. You are no longer welcome in my home, and I shall assume that I am likewise unwelcome in yours. You and I shall be strangers to each other."

"And this is your real opinion! This is your final resolve! Very well, Nephew," cried her ladyship. "I see exactly what you are about, and I shall now know how to act." In this manner, Lady Catherine talked on, until she was at the door, when, turning hastily round, she added, "I take no leave of you, Nephew. You deserve no such attention. I am most seriously displeased."

A row of stately carriages was lined up outside the manor house. A small assembly of Bennet relations stood beside the one in front—the one intended to convey Lydia to Lambton. The remaining carriages were for Lady Catherine and her party. Elizabeth had been wholly surprised to see the other awaiting carriages when she accompanied Lydia outside. Her surprise gave way to unabashed curiosity when Lady Catherine hobbled outside, followed by her humble servant, Mr. Collins. Darcy appeared next with his cousin Anne on his arm. The colonel followed along behind the two of them.

Lydia must have been surprised as well to see another rather distinguished guest was taking her leave from Pemberley amid protest that was not unlike her own. Her mouth agape, she silently stared until she arrested Lady Catherine's attention. Before Lydia could fashion a response that must surely be inappropriate given this new development, Mr. Bennet handed her into the carriage and stepped away. He then signaled Lydia's driver to be on his way.

With Lydia gone, Mr. Bennet escorted his unhappy wife inside the manor house, leaving Elizabeth to join the others. Her eyes questioning, she commenced walking to where Darcy, Anne, and Richard stood.

"Fitzwilliam?"

"Elizabeth, my love, I'm afraid my cousin will be taking leave of Pemberley along with Lady Catherine. However, I have assured her that, unlike her mother, she is always welcome in our home." He looked at Anne and then placed his hand on hers and gave it a gentle squeeze. "Have I not, dearest Cousin?"

"Indeed you have, Cousin."

Elizabeth said, "I trust you had a pleasant stay, Anne, despite all the fuss."

Lady Catherine poked her head outside the carriage. "Come along, Anne. You are wasting your time and mine talking to those two. They are nothing to us now!"

After handing his cousin into the carriage, Darcy and Elizabeth watched as it pulled away. Unlike the colonel, who was in a hurry to get back inside the house, the former two stayed there until Lady Catherine's carriage was completely out of sight. No doubt both were equally pleased to see her gone.

Darcy took his wife by the hand. "I believe we have to prepare for this evening's festivities with the tenants, my love."

"Indeed. Although, now that we have gotten rid of our two most troublesome houseguests, what could possibly go wrong?"

"I do not know, but whatever it might be, I have no doubt we shall persevere, so long as we face it together."

Chapter 9

An Excellent Match

Nine months later ...

By now, Jane and Bingley resided in a neighboring county to Derbyshire. Elizabeth and her dearest sister were happily settled within thirty miles of each other. Even Bingley's sisters were gratified by their brother's move. Mrs. Bennet, on the other hand, was not happy at all to lose the right to boast of her eldest daughter being mistress of such a magnificent estate— its greatest charm being its proximity to Longbourn Village. True, the Bingleys' new home was every bit as grand as Netherfield Park, but who among her circle of friends would ever have a chance to attest to it for themselves?

To Jane and Bingley's dismay, the Wickhams had come for a visit soon after the former took ownership of their new home, and they had been frequent guests ever since. During this most recent visit, the high-spirited couple had been there for weeks with no sign of an imminent leave-taking, despite Bingley's repeated hints for them to be gone.

Elizabeth would not have wished such a fate on anyone, especially the kind-hearted Bingleys, but she could not help feeling that it was better the two of them suffer Lydia and Wickham than Darcy and her. The matter of a different pending visitor filled her head.

"Our guest should be arriving soon," Elizabeth said to her husband.

"What guest is that, my love?"

She raised an exasperated brow.

His question having gone unanswered, he glanced up from his book. He knew that look well. "What did I say?"

"Why, you know very well that we are to entertain Mr. Alston Bingham this evening. Georgiana has been looking forward to his visit all week."

Darcy chose not to dwell on the imminent guest with good reason. He did not like the fellow. Out of nowhere, he had entered the Darcys' life claiming a connection. A cursory investigation of the family line gave proof to his claim. He was indeed a distant cousin.

What a dilemma this entire affair had posed for Darcy. Family meant everything to him. He and Georgiana were not nearly so well acquainted with their Darcy relations as they were with his mother's side of the family. He could no more deny his sister this chance to get to know her third cousin than he would keep her away from the Fitzwilliams.

Darcy said, "You sound as enthusiastic as you profess Georgiana to be. I caution you, however, that, should match-making be your design, you are wasting your time. That gentleman does not stand a chance in the world of winning my sister's hand, regardless of his *connection* to our family, which happens to be the only thing he can boast of."

Such was her husband's opinion. Elizabeth suspected that Georgiana had a different view of the matter. "Is that for you to say, Mr. Darcy?"

"Indeed it is. It is my duty to see that my sister makes an excellent match."

Darcy only wanted the best for his sister. What older brother did not? In this regard, he likened himself very much to his mother-in-law. Just as it was Mrs. Bennet's business in life to make excellent matches for her daughters, so was it his business to do likewise for Georgiana. He wished his sister would understand his reasoning. He had attempted to impress upon her on more than one occasion during their recent time in London the importance of being acquainted with several of the other gentlemen callers. However, Georgiana could only be impressed with her cousin.

His sister was young and naïve, and he feared her feelings for Mr. Bingham might progress from liking to loving with not a care about the young man's ability to keep her in the lifestyle to which she was accustomed. As disheartening as such a prospect was, he expected such fanciful notions from his sister who was more than ten years his junior. He did not expect such sentiments, however, from his wife.

"Would it truly be a bad thing were Georgiana to aspire to a love match? I seem to recall that as the basis of our arrangement, sir."

Elizabeth's reasoning that Darcy himself had enjoyed a love match and therefore Georgiana should be allowed to do the same fell on deaf ears. He was his own master, one of the wealthiest gentlemen in all of Derbyshire. Of course, he decided his own fate. His sister would enjoy no such luxury—that is unless she chose to fall in love with a gentleman of means. As much as he adored his sister and would willing allow her to live out the rest of her days in her beloved family home were she to suffer the unpleasant prospect of spinsterhood, he had no intention of extending such a courtesy to her were she a married woman with an able-bodied husband.

What self-respecting man would abide such an arrangement?

Darcy stood and walked to the window. His hands behind his back, his mind flew to the exact sort of man—George Wickham. Darcy was not unaware that Elizabeth regularly provided funds to that scoundrel by way of her younger sister Lydia. How could he object to how she chose to spend any money she had amassed by the practice of what might be called economy in her own private expenses?

As with every other occasion that Wickham disturbed his thoughts, Darcy released a frustrated breath. It pained him that he would forever refer to a man he loathed as his brother, especially since he had managed to avoid such an unpleasant prospect when he arrived in Ramsgate all those years back and saved his sister Georgiana from eloping with the wicked man.

He meant to rid his life of George Wickham forever, and he thought he had done it. Then he met and fell in love with Elizabeth. Indeed, he and Elizabeth were together when she learned her youngest sister had run off with that scoundrel. The pain in her eyes was such that he never wished to see again. Silently vowing to protect her, he did everything in his power to recover her youngest sister. He did not know at the time that it would be a means of uniting them—even though he thought only of her in doing so, he did not know what it would mean for his own felicity.

Having George Wickham as a brother was a terrible fate indeed, but he would not change a thing in that regard for his prize was Elizabeth's hand in marriage.

Elizabeth said, "Perhaps all this worrying is for naught. The young man has not declared his intentions toward Georgiana, after all."

"Indeed, he has not. I strongly suspect his lapse is owing to a lack of opportunity. It will be my responsibility to see that he never gets one."

For Georgiana's part, she still could not believe her cousin was actually in Derbyshire—staying in Lambton and now expected to arrive at Pemberley at any moment. Of all the gentlemen she enjoyed meeting the most during her coming out Season, Georgiana's imagination, as well as her fancy, had been captured by Mr. Bingham. She had been intrigued from the moment their eyes met across a crowded room. His look was vaguely familiar to her. Something about his gaze gave her a warm indication of his kindness of heart.

He had been in attendance at every ball that she attended. He was a patron of the theater and an ardent lover of fine art. He could spend hours discussing books. Everything he did he did very well, be it dancing, reciting poetry, even composing. What was more; he was blessed with all the best parts of beauty with his tall person, amazing grey eyes, and amiable mien.

The most agreeable thing about him was that he was of Darcy lineage. Indeed, his grandfather and Georgiana's grandfather were brothers, the former being a younger son. As such, he had taken his family to the south of England in pursuit of his fortune. However, he had returned to Pemberley with his family on many occasions, as relations were wont to do. His daughter, Agatha Bingham nee Darcy, Mr. Bingham's mother, had retained such a favorable impression of her days of youth. She had imparted her only child with so many happy memories of the manor house, the woods, and Derbyshire in general that her memories were akin to his own, even though he had yet to visit Pemberley himself.

His mother had married a gentleman in trade, a Mr. Wentworth Bingham. What few ties she had with the Darcys of Pemberley had been severed several decades past as a result. How embarrassed Georgiana had been to learn that such callousness had been afforded to someone of her own blood generations earlier. She could not have been happier to make her distant cousin's acquaintance. Were it solely up to her, she would accept Mr. Bingham into the family fold with open arms.

If only her brother suffered a modicum of the pleasure of making the acquaintance of his distant cousin then Georgiana would have had no reason at all to repine. Her brother had always been overprotective of her, especially after the Ramsgate affair. She could not truly fault him in that. However, she was of an age where she would be expected to choose a husband—to begin her life under someone other than her brother's protection.

He will have to come to grips with that eventually, and he might as well start now. Here, Georgiana sighed. Once again, she was getting ahead of herself. Her cousin was a worldly man of sense and education. He had a charming, engaging manner. She was sure he could have his choice of any woman in the *ton*. By his own account, he was a man of independent means that afforded him a life that she could not but admire, for he was an artist— rather, an aspiring artist on the verge of making a name for himself.

Their shared lineage had drawn them together. Their mutual appreciation of art bound them to each other. Fulfilling his promise to teach her a thing or two about the subtler techniques of oil painting, the two of them began to spend time with each other while in town. She had Mrs. Annesley's timely habit of dozing off while reading to thank for a rather titillating lesson one afternoon.

The three of them were in the garden. Mr. Bingham and Georgiana were standing at an easel admiring her work and Mrs. Annesley sat a respectable distance away, reading a book. The place where the former two stood afforded a perfect view of the aging companion.

The closer he stood to her the louder her heart thumped against her chest. The touch of his fingers against hers sent frissons of excitement through her body when he reached for the paintbrush with the intention of demonstrating a different lighting technique. Their eyes fixed upon each other's, he commenced stroking, not looking at what he was doing. At times, he stood even closer, close enough for her to appreciate his masculinity, his broad shoulders, and his virile, aromatic scent.

Georgiana was young, but she knew when a man was flirting with her. A year or so prior, she might have objected. Of course, that was before she had come out and a measure of protest was the proper thing to do. However, she was now a woman who knew what it meant to have a man look at her the way Mr. Bingham looked at her, and she liked it.

Only one man had looked at her like that before—George Wickham. What a fool she had been then to think his intentions toward her had been honorable. However, Mr. Bingham was no George Wickham. Her cousin was no scoundrel who would be tempted by her dowry of thirty thousand pounds and no one could persuade her otherwise.

Her cousin and she were of the same blood and, as best she could tell, of the same temperament with similar likes and dislikes. Most of all, they liked each other and they could spend hours talking to each other. The fact that he was family (albeit distant) afforded him a measure of liberty that others did not enjoy. What's more, he had garnered Elizabeth's approval, which, in and of itself, was a good thing, for she had a way with Darcy that others lacked, even Georgiana herself. Her good opinion alone was enough to cause Darcy to relax his guard a little when Mr. Bingham called.

The one thing that Darcy had not allowed was an invitation for Mr. Bingham to dine at Darcy House. However, his being in Lambton was another thing. Darcy could not possibly refuse the man who had given so many hints of longing to see his own grandfather's birthplace—the place he had dreamed of seeing for the better part of his life.

Chapter 10

According to Plan

His eyes widened to take in all the splendor that stretched before him. Having done everything in his power to ingratiate himself into Miss Georgiana Darcy's life during the London Season, he sent a letter to Pemberley informing the Darcys he was visiting the area and staying in Lambton soon after his arrival. Just as he had anticipated, an invitation to dine at Pemberley was extended forthwith.

Finally, he was at the one place that had occupied his thoughts for the better part of a decade—Pemberley. It was a remarkable sight, exciting the artist's imagination beyond measure.

What a place this is—its natural beauty entirely preserved, not counteracted by an awkward taste. Then he espied Pemberley's crowning jewel—the manor house. A large, stone building, it stood well on rising ground and was backed by a ridge of high, woody hills. In front of it was a flowing stream—its banks neither formally nor falsely adorned. He could spend months, if not years, capturing the beauty of such a place for generations of people to behold. He secretly planned to do just that.

Relying on his cousin's affectionate heart to empathize with his plight, he had often spoken of his desire to visit his mother's family home. How fortuitous Miss Darcy had considered it was upon learning that he was planning a tour of the North that summer.

"You must be sure to visit Pemberley when you are there," she had said.

"I believe I could be prevailed on to do so. I confess that seeing the place my beloved grandfather once called home is a most pleasing prospect. Not to mention what a great pleasure it would give me to spend time with you."

Bingham knew that Fitzwilliam Darcy would not be keen on the idea of his only sister aligning herself with a struggling, or rather an aspiring, artist, despite the family connection. His best option would be to spend time with her outside of her brother's watchful eyes—to woo her—to make her fall in love with him, and then Darcy would have to go along with the scheme.

When he arrived at the house, he received a warm welcoming reception from Mrs. Darcy and Miss

Darcy. The master of the house was part of the welcoming party as well, but Bingham was not entirely convinced that Darcy was pleased to receive him.

Now there he was, sitting in the drawing room at Pemberley, trying his best to put a picture to those things he had heard his beloved mother speak about all those years ago—the stuff of fairytales even to a young boy's ears. *People truly live this way,* he thought, looking around the room in awe of Pemberley's grandeur.

His eyes landed upon another person who had been an unknowing champion of his cause—Mrs. Elizabeth Darcy. Having made her acquaintance in London, as well, he knew his plans would not stand a chance of coming to fruition were he to lose her good opinion. *Her husband is clearly in her power else I most certainly would not be sitting here.*

His thoughts drifted five miles away to the other members of his traveling party: Angelica and little Gabriel. His parting words to the former were fresh in his mind. *Have patience, my dear. Everything is all happening according to plan.*

The time to put the next step into action was near. *I shall invite Georgiana and Elizabeth to meet Angelica on the morrow. No doubt, the three ladies will get along swimmingly. It is absolutely necessary that they do.*

Before the evening drew to a close, Bingham and Georgiana were at liberty to speak privately. "Miss Darcy," he said, "I have to tell you about a new development in my life since I made your acquaintance in London. Actually, it is not a new development in its entirety. I led you to believe I had no immediate family when such is not the case. You see, I feared if you knew about my sister and her *situation* you might be put off."

Georgiana clasped her hands to her bosom in eager excitement. "You have a sister, sir? I have another cousin whose acquaintance I have yet to make?"

"Well, yes. I have a sister—rather a half-sister. I have only recently made her acquaintance myself. She is my late father's daughter—his illegitimate daughter. She is recently widowed, and, what's more, there is an infant child. When she came to me with her story and tangible proof of her claims, I could not turn her away. Family means everything to me—just as it does to you. You and I are very much alike in that way, are we not?"

Georgiana's smile encouraged him to go on.

"Her name is Angelica—Mrs. Angelica Carter. Knowing her plight, I thought I owed it to her to become her protector."

"It was indeed the honorable thing to do, sir. I am sorry for her dire circumstances and that society may not embrace her because of them. You need not suffer concern that I would bestow her any unkindness. I would very much like to meet her, and I am sure I speak correctly for my sister Elizabeth in saying that she would enjoy meeting Mrs. Carter as well."

~~~

Having settled it that the ladies from Pemberley would visit Angelica the very next day after learning about her existence, Bingham resolved that neither he nor Angelica would be away from the inn the whole of the morning.

He rightly surmised that this meeting was to be a trial for Angelica, for she was very shy. The idea of meeting strangers held no appeal to her at all, and certainly not *these* strangers. Her lack of fondness for high society in particular bothered him exceedingly. She would have to grow accustomed to it. Their world was changing and all for the better.

Angelica, for her part, was walking back and forth wearing a new pattern in the rug, and when she was not doing that she was sitting beside the fireplace half attending her book. The sound of a carriage drew Bingham and Angelica to the window, and they saw two elegant ladies being handed down to the street. Bingham immediately recognized the livery, and he placed his hand on Angelica's shoulder. She was so anxious she jumped.

"You must calm yourself, my dear," he began, "you will find Mrs. Darcy and Miss Darcy to be charming and wholly lacking in pretension despite the stately carriage on the street below and their elegant attire."

Minutes later, the visitors appeared, and the formidable introduction took place. With astonishment, Georgiana discerned that her new acquaintance, a fair-haired young woman, was at least as embarrassed as she was. Also to Georgiana's surprise, she detected that the young woman was every ounce as shy as she was. Thus, the two ladies were contented to allow Elizabeth and Mr. Bingham to carry out the bulk of the conversation.

Looking to discern a family resemblance between the half-siblings, Georgiana's eyes wandered from Mr. Bingham's face to Angelica's. Finding none, she contented herself with the idea that Angelica must derive her looks from her mother's family. That must be the case, for Mr. Bingham's resemblance to the Darcy line of the family was unmistakable. Angelica was tall and on a scale comparable to Georgiana. She was not as handsome as Mr. Bingham, but Georgiana knew herself well enough to imagine no one could possibly possess all the makings of perfection as those embodied in her cousin. It was all she could do not to look at him. When she did look, his eyes were invariably fixed on Angelica. His affection for her was undeniable.

They had not been long together before Elizabeth said, "I was sorry to hear about the recent loss of your husband, Mrs. Carter. You have my condolences."

Coloring a bit, Angelica nodded her appreciation of the avowal. When some mention was made of the child, Angelica grew slightly more animated. Perhaps aggravated was a more apt description of her sentiments. She really wanted the visitors to be on their way.

"The babe is asleep," she said with energy. "Neither of us slept well last night. He was quite fussy. You see he is getting a new tooth."

"Oh, then we will not keep you any longer than we must," said Elizabeth, who did not mean to overstay her welcome.

When the guests were gone, Angelica resumed pacing the floor. Bingham walked behind her and placed his hands about her shoulders. "Pray what is the matter?"

"I wish I could be as calm as you are, but I am not so naïve when it comes to women as you are."

"What is that supposed to mean? I am certain Georgiana adores you already."

"Perhaps she does, but what of her sister? That woman has a very critical eye."

"As far as anyone knows, you are my sister. I shall do nothing in public to give anyone cause to suppose otherwise." He took her in his arms and kissed her face. "You never need worry. I shall always be here for you and Gabriel. You must trust me."

"You know how much I abhor such pretense." Escaping his embrace, she cried, "I hate these drab mourning clothes. I hate wearing my hair in this dreadful manner. The lies, the schemes, I hate all of it. Why can't we return to the way things were before you got it into your head to seek out your mother's relations? Were we not happy then?"

"You know very well that I am ill-suited to the life of a commoner—scraping out a living and scarcely able to make ends meet. I am of Darcy lineage. I was meant to live the life of a gentleman but for my mother's ill-advised choices. Such a manner of living suits me in every way. And now, when I have it all within my grasp, I will not allow anything or anyone to deter me."

Chapter 11

His Touch

The next day brought news that Mr. Bingham would be a frequent visitor at Pemberley owing to his offer to paint Georgiana's portrait. This did not sit well with Darcy. "It seems a bit too convenient for my taste."

When Bingham informed Georgiana he wished to paint her portrait, and Georgiana told Elizabeth, Elizabeth immediately approved the scheme. *What is the harm?* Elizabeth considered. Her sister would be under Mrs. Annesley's supervision during the sessions, and it afforded time for Mr. Bingham and Georgiana to get better acquainted. Also, the young man's reasoning had been sound. Being able to boast of painting Miss Georgiana Darcy's portrait, even if pro bono, would mean a great deal for an aspiring artist, he had said. Surely such a claim would open doors that would otherwise be closed to him.

What was deemed agreeable to Elizabeth met with a healthy measure of skepticism on Darcy's part. What a ruse this was in his estimation. He told his wife as much.

"What do you mean?" Elizabeth asked.

"His desire to capture Georgiana's likeness is little more than an excuse to ingratiate himself with our family."

"Lest you forget, the gentleman *is* a member of the family."

"Being the grandson of the brother of my father's father barely warrants the right to trade on the connection."

"What say you that we refer to him as your grandfather's brother's grandson—that's rather more personal, is it not? Better still, what say you that we refer to him as your third cousin? Were Pemberley entailed, Mr. Bingham might even boast of being a possible heir."

"Thank heavens Pemberley is not entailed, for knowing him, as I strongly suspect I do, he would certainly endeavor to lay claim to it."

"You are entirely too severe on the young man. I see no harm in his wishing to establish a greater connection to his family. Save a half-sister and her child, he is all alone in this world. Besides, Georgiana will be perfectly safe in his company. Mrs. Annesley will be present during the sittings."

Reluctantly conceding his wife's point, Darcy said, "So long as the two of them remain in Mrs. Annesley's company, I suppose there is no harm. He is her—" Darcy gave a slight roll of his eyes to the ceiling "—*our* cousin."

Elizabeth smiled. "Georgiana will be pleased."

"And what exactly will you be doing during these calls?" Darcy asked, his mood improving.

"There is any number of things I might do. There are the regular visits to the tenant families, daily letter writing—"

"—Spending time with me?" Darcy interrupted. "Where does that fall on your list?"

Her own spirits rising to playfulness, she said, "Where on my list would you like it to fall?"

Placing his finger on her lips, he slowly trailed it to her heart. "Here, my love."

Nearly two years of marriage and his touch still did things to her. A powerful sense of yearning for the man she knew was hers and hers alone flooded her being. Her desire fully awakened, she moistened her lips. " Your point is well taken," she replied, placing her hand on his cheek and encouraging him to lean forward and his lips to meet hers.

Elsewhere, Georgiana was seeing her cousin off. The two of them ambled across the black and white marble tiled floor. By his expression, Bingham was still very much in awe of the manor house. It was all he could do to tear his eyes away from the majestic ceiling paintings.

Making every effort to claim her share of his attention, Georgiana said, "As happy as I am to sit for you, the notion of you painting my portrait for free is unthinkable. It is not as though my brother does not have the means to reward you amply."

"No doubt, he does. However, unless he approaches me with such an offer, I do not think it would be wise for me to solicit him. He might then exercise the option of saying no, which would hamper my cause exceedingly."

Crumpling her brow, she replied, "How so, if I might ask?"

"Surely you know that I wish to paint you so that we might spend time with each other."

Georgiana felt the color spread all over her body. She had been exceedingly careful not to show any of her gentleman admirers any manner of favoritism during her coming out Season in town. It was somehow different with Mr. Bingham. Her attraction to him was beyond her power to resist.

He was not at all like the others—with all their wealth and heralded connections. How insufficient were these things in garnering Georgiana's favor. In a sense, she was just as ignorant of her family's history as he was. Perhaps, when her daily sittings were over, they might have the excuse of spending time in the library poring through old family records, she considered.

Indeed, the prospect of spending time in his company was appealing in every possible way. She found herself agreeing with him. Why risk her brother rejecting the notion of his capturing Georgiana's likeness on canvas by asking for some sort of compensation?

Mr. Bingham and Georgiana were together in the music room early the next day. Mrs. Annesley was present as well—close enough to keep an observant eye on the couple, but not so close as to hear whatever was being said between them.

Not that it mattered, for all of Mr. Bingham's focus was on his work. Georgiana, when she was not doing everything in her power to maintain the pose he had suggested for his masterpiece, was pleasantly engaged in fanciful imaginings involving her cousin.

They were the sort of imaginings that she knew to keep to herself. Her brother would not approve of Mr. Bingham despite the family connection and Georgiana reasoned it was solely because of her cousin's lack of fortune.

Is it Mr. Bingham's fault that he was not born into wealth, the likes of which my brother and I have always known? To Georgiana's way of thinking, her cousin had just as much right to avail himself of Pemberley's largess as did Fitzwilliam and she. His own grandfather had called Pemberley his home.

Would it be a crime for Mr. Bingham to know that same feeling? For his children? Our children?

There I go again—assuming affection where prevailing evidence supports there is none, she silently berated herself. On the other hand, she ought not to be too hard on herself for secretly falling in love with her third cousin. She threw a furtive glance at the object of her musings. His masculine beauty never ceased to amaze her.

Just then, he looked up from the canvas and saw that Georgiana was looking at him. His eyes, though devastatingly charming, held a gentle admonishment that she needed to resume her former pose.

Indeed, she was in grave danger of falling deeply in love with her cousin. She hoped that, in spending so much time with her, his feelings would one day assume a similar vein. Only time would tell. In the meantime, she knew enough about her brother's wishes for her future marital felicity to know she had better not show any symptom of love for Mr. Bingham to anyone. Whatever were his sentiments toward her, be they of a familial, a platonic, or a romantic persuasion, she wanted to spend as much time getting to know him as possible. Any suspicion of affection between them on her brother's part would be the surest means of sending Mr. Bingham on his way.

Chapter 12

State of Mind

D arcy arrived at Matlock early in response to an urgent missive from his aunt Lady Ellen, dispatched on the earl's behest. The elderly man had suffered a bout of apoplexy. With his son and heir, Lord Robert Fitzwilliam, on the continent and his younger son, Colonel Richard Fitzwilliam, on a secret assignment, he wanted Darcy to understand the inner workings of his affairs in their absence.

With the curtains drawn, Lord Edward Fitzwilliam's room was dark, at first giving Darcy to wonder if he had made it in time, or whether his uncle had perished. Glancing to his left, Darcy espied his uncle being attended by the family's physician. His lordship waved his nephew to come closer. "I was beginning to think you might not arrive in time. Well, let us get on with it." The earl's voice sounded frail and weak, not at all like that of the man who wore his pride in being the titular head of the Fitzwilliam family on his sleeve. "In my eldest son's absence, it will be your responsibility to look after the family once I am gone."

After a cursory glance at the physician and a slight bow, Darcy pulled up a chair beside the bed and took a seat. "You should not speak this way, Uncle. I am confident your current malady is little more than a minor setback. You will survive all of us. You are far too stubborn to do otherwise."

"I might have thought as much myself at this time last week, but an inconvenient fit of apoplexy has a way of changing a man's perspective. I am subject to go at any moment." The earl started coughing uncontrollably. The physician, who had been tidying his things in preparation to leave when Darcy entered the room, stopped what he was doing, poured water into a glass, and held it to the earl's mouth, encouraging him to take slow sips.

Once he had calmed, Lord Fitzwilliam said, "You are aware that my elder son Robert is on the continent. We have not heard a word from him in months. Richard is off on a secret campaign, the nature of which even I have not been made privy to. My steward is a good man, but he cannot be expected to carry on in my absence. The task falls squarely on your shoulders, Nephew, at least until the viscount returns. Even then I will need you to help him along. He is woefully ill-prepared to ascend to the earldom."

Here again, the earl started coughing. This time, Darcy picked up the glass and coaxed him to drink. "I shall do what I can, Uncle. For the time being, you must calm yourself. Rest for now. I shall be here when you awaken."

"Rest! All I have done for the past few days is rest. This business will not wait. Listen carefully for there are vital concerns you ought to know."

Darcy's aunt, Lady Ellen, came into the room. The elegant woman, who after more than five decades on Earth continued to have more than her fair share of beauty, walked over to the bed and sat by her husband.

"How is our patient?"

Darcy gave her a knowing look. She had warned him of her husband's determination to put his affairs in order even though the doctor had proclaimed his worries were greatly premature.

The earl said, "I have been explaining to my nephew how he will in effect be the head of the family until our elder son is found."

"What attempts have been made to locate Robert?" Darcy asked, directing the question to her ladyship.

"Several letters have been dispatched to places on his itinerary. I believe it is only a matter of time before he is located and he returns home."

Her ladyship commenced fussing over her husband, who wanted none of it; thus giving Darcy a moment to reflect on what was happening at Pemberley. Time spent at Matlock would be time away from Elizabeth. They were no longer newlyweds, but still they had not been parted from each other for a single night since the wedding.

The thought of asking her to join him in Matlock did cross his mind once or twice, but he did not want to interrupt the good work she was doing with Pemberley's tenants. Also, asking Elizabeth to join him meant asking Georgiana to accompany them as well.

He had seen the progress Bingham was making on his sister's portrait. The gentleman did indeed possess great promise. Perhaps being able to boast of capturing Georgiana's likeness was just the feather in his cap the man needed to set about on the road to fame and fortune. Removing Georgiana from Pemberley would merely serve to delay the progress that had been made. The last thing he wanted was to be the means of Bingham remaining in Derbyshire a moment longer than was necessary. While it was true that his sister enjoyed being acquainted with their distant cousin exceedingly, Darcy was as determined as ever that nothing would become of it. In fact, whenever he was at leisure to think about it, the idea of an artist claiming his sister's hand was enough to make him laugh aloud.

Sadly, this is not one of those times, Darcy considered, fixing his gaze on the earl. However grave was his uncle's condition, the older man was serious in his convictions to put his affairs in order. As family meant everything to Darcy, he intended to do everything in his power to ease his uncle's state of mind.

~~~

Some days later, Elizabeth was riding along in a horse-drawn carriage early one morning, still in the afterglow of shared intimacies with Darcy. They did not spend nearly so much time with each other now that his uncle had fallen ill and Darcy was spending so much time traveling back and forth between the two great estates.

Elizabeth would not complain. She had more than enough causes to occupy her days. She might also have had the excuse of occasionally calling on her neighbors, but she took very little pleasure in such excursions. She may have been seen by some as an *old* married woman by now, and she may have been expected to comport herself accordingly, but she was barely three and twenty. None of the Derbyshire society women of her acquaintance were on the best side of five and forty, or so it seemed to her. Growing up with four sisters, Elizabeth always enjoyed the company of her own sex. When she was not with her sisters, she could often be found with her intimate friend Charlotte.

Those were the days, she silently waxed poetically. That was the one drawn back to Mr. Bingham's near constant presence at Pemberley of late: his command of the best part of Georgiana's days. Again, Elizabeth would not complain, for Georgiana liked spending time with her newfound cousin too much for Elizabeth to begrudge the loss of her companionship. *Besides,* she considered, *Georgiana will one day marry and leave the fold despite my husband's secret wish to put it off for the indeterminate future.*

The carriage drew to a halt in front of the little cottage belonging to a Mr. and Mrs. Brown, recalling Elizabeth to her purpose. This was just the first stop of at least three that she had planned for that morning. The last would be a visit to the Pollards' home, a rather lively household with five daughters ranging in ages from five to fifteen, a mother who fancied herself of a nervous persuasion, and a father who spent nearly every waking hour away from home endeavoring to provide for all of them.

Were Elizabeth called upon to do so, of the scores of Pemberley's tenants, she would have to say that she liked this particular family most of all. Of course, the Pollard family's circumstances were too unfortunate for their situation to be compared to her former life at Longbourn. However, given the liveliness of so many members of the fairer sex competing for their share of attention at any given moment, Elizabeth was afforded a measure of comfort she sometimes forgot how much she missed.

~~~

On the following Wednesday, the Bingleys eluded their houseguests and visited the Darcys at Pemberley. It did not take long for the ladies to leave their husbands to their own devices and set off for a walk on a wooded path. Of all the subjects the two sisters might have discussed, nothing was more urgent than the matter of Jane and her husband's discord.

Jane said, "In many respects, the situation is worse than being at Netherfield because not only is there Caroline to deal with but also the Wickhams. They are always engaged in one disagreement or another, and Charles—well you know how much he hates arguments and conflict as you may very well remember from the earliest days at Netherfield when you and Darcy were getting to—"

Here Jane paused and cleared her throat, "Ahem—getting acquainted, and so he throws up his hands. I am left to play peacekeeper, and, well frankly, I am rather tired of it all. I simply wish they would all just leave us alone."

"Bravo Jane, I think that is the second most severe speech that I ever heard you utter," Elizabeth exclaimed—the first being when Jane had cited the Bingley sisters' feigned approbation toward her upon first making their acquaintance.

"Indeed, that is our purpose in being here at Pemberley today."

"If a clash between the Wickhams and Miss Bingley has been the means of your being here, I have to tell you that I owe them a debt of gratitude. We do not see each other nearly so much as I would like."

"Indeed. Pray how do you get along with the newest member of your family?"

"Ah! Mr. Bingham. I must say we get along very well. Georgiana is quite taken with him. There is a little wonder, for the gentleman really is quite charming. My husband does not agree. On some levels, I suspect he views his cousin as a competitor for Georgiana's esteem. I posit he suffers an unwillingness to admit that his sister is no longer a young girl who needs his constant protection but rather a young woman on the precipice of forming her own acquaintances and connections."

"After what happened at Ramsgate, you can hardly blame him for his fierce protectiveness toward his sister." Jane colored. "Oh, Lizzy, I suppose I ought not to have said anything. I certainly did not intend to touch upon a subject that might give you pain."

"All that unfolded many years ago. Georgiana is not that same girl. She has grown into a sensible, intelligent young woman who is ready to take her place in society. How can she do that if he will not allow her a bit more freedom?"

Later that same day, Elizabeth and Georgiana were together in the library. Elizabeth's talk with Jane was weighing on her mind, She thought she ought to discuss the matter with Georgiana. "Pray how is your portrait coming along?"

"I wish I could say, but Mr. Bingham will not allow me to have a glimpse of what he is doing."

"I am not surprised to hear that. I imagine that is the way with artists; unwilling to share their masterpieces with anyone until the unveiling."

"That is what he says in response to my daily entreaties. On the one hand, I can hardly wait to see it, but then again, I am not particularly eager."

"Oh!" Elizabeth exclaimed. "Why do you espouse the latter sentiment?"

"Once he is finished capturing my likeness, he will have no reason to remain here in Derbyshire, I am afraid. He must be off in pursuit of his passion for his profession. I am not unaware of the sacrifice he has made in remaining here for so long even though I have offered to compensate him using what little money I have at my own disposal, but he will not hear of it." Georgiana bit her lower lip. "My brother has yet to commission a master to capture your likeness. Perhaps you might persuade him to engage Mr. Bingham's services. Then my cousin shall have cause to remain in Derbyshire even longer, which would please me exceedingly."

Elizabeth suspected such a plea would be wasted on her husband. Darcy did not like Bingham any more now than he did when he first met him, despite the family connection and Bingham's wont to do and say all the things that ought to garner Darcy's approbation whenever the two were in company.

"Georgiana, I do not think it would be my place to suggest such a thing to my husband."

"Who is better than you to do it? I know it is beyond his power to deny you anything. I just know that given a sufficient passage of time, my cousin will come to realize that his lack of fortune means nothing to me, and that I—" Here, the young lady halted her impassioned plea.

"What were you about to say, Georgiana? I know you have a very favorable opinion of your cousin, one he is not unworthy of, I am sure. Is there more than merely a fond attachment on your part?"

"Oh, Elizabeth! The more time I spend in my cousin's company, the more I am persuaded that he is the only man in the world for me. I love him." She smiled as though this were the first time she had spoken those words aloud. "I love him," she repeated. "It is my ardent wish that he will one day feel the same about me."

Knowing how Darcy would react should he learn his sister's feelings had progressed from liking to loving in so short a duration, Elizabeth could not help but suffer a measure of foreboding. Her husband meant for his sister to marry a man of consequence—a man with the means of keeping her in the manner of living in which she had been reared.

Georgiana pursed her lips. She had just confessed her heart's most closely kept secret to Elizabeth, whom she admired and esteemed, and this was the response she was to receive. Silence. She said, "I am surprised by your reaction, Elizabeth. You must have something to say to me."

"Finding one's self in love is often a cause for joy. However, in this particular case, I feel it would be a disservice to you were I to congratulate you for suffering such sentiments."

"How can you say such a thing? You have always been one of Mr. Bingham's staunchest supporters. Were it not for your generosity of spirit toward him, he would never have been allowed to visit Pemberley and learn about his family. Our acquaintance with him would have ended soon after our first introduction in London. Why have you turned against him?"

"Georgiana, I have not turned against him at all. I value family above everything, and thus I was eager to do my part in uniting yours."

"Then why does the idea of my falling in love with him give you displeasure? Is it his lack of fortune?"

"I would never judge a man by his financial worth. It is not that at all."

"Is it my brother? Has he thoroughly poisoned you against the idea of a union between my cousin and me?"

"Pray let us not have this discussion, which we both can agree is premature at best and likely unwarranted in its entirety. I do not mean to diminish the import of your affections for your cousin, but there is no evidence to support that he returns those feelings ... unless there is something more that you have not told me. Has he done or said anything which might lead you to suspect his feelings for you are based upon anything but familial affection?"

Not wishing to admit to all the intimate encounters she and her cousin had shared out of fear of being deemed as wanton, Georgiana held her tongue.

"Has he?" Elizabeth repeated.

"No—he has not. However, you ought to know that should Mr. Bingham offer his hand to me, I will not hesitate to accept it. Neither my brother's sentiments to the contrary nor the opposing opinions of anyone else will dissuade me."

"It pains me to hear you speak this way." Elizabeth's stance was not so liberal and encouraging now as it had been when she had spoken with Jane earlier. Although she could never think so little of Mr. Bingham as did her husband, Elizabeth could not deny her increasing concern. Mr. Bingham and Georgiana were spending far too much time in each other's company of late—time not always spent creating his masterpiece, but Elizabeth did not witness any symptom of love on his part the likes of which Georgiana suffered toward him. It would be a mistake for Georgiana to set herself up for disappointment and heartbreak when he took his leave of Derbyshire. She told Georgiana as much.

Georgiana said, "Are we not all capable of making mistakes? Imagine if my brother had held your fondness for George Wickham against you?"

"I beg your pardon?" Elizabeth beseeched.

"Do you deny that George was once considered by many who know you best to be your particular favorite? Did you not at one time consider him a better man than my brother? I say this not to judge you, but to point out that we are all but mere human beings and subject to the same human frailties."

"Indeed, we all make mistakes, but that does not stand to reason that we ought to willfully dismiss the council of those who only mean to protect us. That is precisely your brother's intention. It is my intention as well. Do anything but forget what you are about."

~~~

Georgiana and Mr. Bingham had finished the morning session and were now enjoying a walk on her favorite path before he was to take his leave. Darcy had stayed the night in Matlock, and Elizabeth was visiting a tenant's wife who was bed-ridden after having given birth to her first child.

Georgiana's mind was intently engaged in thoughts of all that had unfolded between her cousin and her both in London as well as at Pemberley. She was convinced she was in a fair way of knowing all there was to know about the inner workings of his heart and what it would mean for her future.

His voice pierced her private musings. "Would it disappoint you to know that when you and I are apart, I spend most of my time secretly crafting another portrait of you?"

Comfortable with him, she laced her arm through his. "Why would I be disappointed? I am indeed flattered. Has Mrs. Carter seen it?"

"No—no one has seen it. You see, I am agreeably engaged in capturing your likeness in my mind—for my eyes only, as it were. You, in all your magnificent splendor, just as nature intended."

Georgiana felt an all too familiar blush spread over her body. The implication of his speech was clear. He imagined her nude. As scandalous as his saying such a thing was, she could not object. Not when he was looking at her the way he was—that way a man looked at a woman whom he desired and the way a woman wanted to be looked at by the man whom she adored.

Bingham swept his arm around her waist and drew her closer. He traced his fingers along her neckline, her chin, and then her lips.

He leaned his head down. She closed her eyes. His warm breath against her skin invited her lips apart.

"I believe it is time," he whispered softly in her ear, "that I declare my intentions toward you to your brother."

Somewhat surprised, she opened her eyes. Her heartbeat thumping against her chest, she said, "And what exactly are your intentions, sir?"

Releasing his hand from her waist, he took her hand in his and raised it to his lips. Turning it over, he kissed her palm. Looking deep into her eyes, he said, "Can there be any doubt in your mind, my dearest Georgiana?"

Chapter 13

Untold Unhappiness

Darcy paced the floor. He'd known it would one day come to this. He was no more in favor of such an unequal alliance now than he was months ago. His sister deserved better than such a man as Alston Bingham.

"What will it take to convince you that I love your sister?"

"Time will tell. Assuming I would consent to your proposal, what are your plans for providing for my sister, especially in light of the fact that you have your sister and her child to care for?"

"I am not without means, sir, if that is your only objection. I have my own income from my inheritance from my mother."

What a meager inheritance it is at five thousand pounds, Bingham considered. *The income on that amount is nothing in comparison to Darcy's, but Georgiana's thirty thousand pounds will go a long way in elevating my financial standing. One day Angelica might draw the attention of a wealthy benefactor as well. True, I would not like it, but I would learn to tolerate it for the greater good.*

"I do not claim that I will be able to keep your sister in the style of living to which she has been accustomed all her life. There will be sacrifices. Your sister is aware of all of this."

Sitting alone in the parlor, Georgiana waited. Upon seeing Mr. Bingham speaking quietly with her brother and then subsequently following him out of the room, Georgiana's agitation was extreme. She truly feared her brother's disapprobation, for he had not warmed to the idea of Mr. Bingham being a third cousin. Surely the prospect of now having to call him his brother would be a cause for untold unhappiness. She deserved a husband of consequence in the world, her brother would argue. Of course, her brother would rant and rave to that very effect, but, in the end of it all, he would relent. Having chosen a love match for himself, how could he not allow her the same liberty?

She sat in misery until Mr. Bingham appeared again, when, looking at him, she grew a little concerned about his comportment. In under a minute, he approached the table where she was sitting and said in a whisper, "Your brother wishes to see you."

She did not like his look or his tone, and she wondered what her brother had said to cause such a dismal turn of her dear cousin's countenance. Arising from her seat, she said, "Mr. Bingham—"

"—Speak with your brother. I shall call on you early in the morning at the usual time." With that, he bowed and went on his way, leaving a rather befuddled young lady standing there.

Darcy was walking about the room, looking grave and anxious, when his sister entered. "Georgiana," said he, "what are you doing? What are you thinking in accepting this man? You hardly even know him."

She hated distressing her beloved brother by her choice and filling him with uncertainty and fear, but this was her decision. She tried her best to assure him of her attachment to her cousin. Theirs was not an attraction of a few days or even a few months, but one of knowing rooted in their shared passions as well as lineage.

"I am sorry to say that I do not bestow my blessing, at least not willingly. I do not believe it is in your best interests. However, if you are determined to have him then I am willing to reconsider my position on the condition of an extended engagement period."

"What do you expect will change?"

"A great deal might change or nothing at all. Certainly there is no harm in waiting, is there?"

"What are you suggesting?"

"If you are old enough to marry you ought to be old enough to have some indication," he said. It pained him to utter those words, but his sister was not a child, and there was the fact that the cousins had been spending a great deal of time together of late.

As aggrieved as she was to hear her brother, whom she likened to a father, speak this way, the implication of his speech did not escape her. Georgiana colored. "Mr. Bingham is a consummate gentleman, as you would very well discern if you would but spend more time getting to know him."

"That is my point. I know nothing about him that would allow me to relish the prospect of his taking you away to parts unknown to suffer life as the wife of a struggling—I beg your pardon—an *aspiring* artist."

"You have not given yourself the trouble of knowing him. You have been opposed to the idea of his getting acquainted with his own mother's family—our family—almost from the moment he informed you of the connection."

"I will not have you speak to me in this manner, young lady. It is for me to decide whom you shall marry and whom you see for that matter. Be thankful that I have allowed that gentleman to spend time with you at all."

Oh! You are impossible. How on Earth have I managed to convince myself otherwise all these years? Georgiana thought but did not voice aloud. Elizabeth, of whom Georgiana had the highest opinion of in the world, would very likely have expressed so unguarded a view. However, through her sister's instruction, she began to comprehend that a woman may take liberties with her husband that a brother will not always allow in a sister more than ten years younger than himself. She did have the liberty of storming out of the room and inconveniencing him by leaving the door standing wide open, which is precisely what she did.

After spending time with Georgiana and listening to her account of Darcy's decision, Elizabeth sought her husband's company. "I spoke with Georgiana," she began the instant she came across him. "She is terribly upset."

"I am not surprised to hear that."

"I understand that you are requiring a lengthy passage of time before you will give your consent for her to be married to Mr. Bingham with the goal of allowing them more time to get acquainted with each other."

He shrugged. "I am hoping that the results of my investigations into the man's past will yield information that will prove my suspicions are either legitimate or wholly unfounded."

"So this delay is not to give Georgiana and Mr. Bingham more time to get acquainted, but to give you more time to investigate the gentleman."

"Indeed."

"This smacks of subterfuge on your part—dare I call it duplicity? Have you not boasted that disguise of any sort is your abhorrence? Are you above practicing that which you preach?"

"It is my sister's future that is at stake. You know there is nothing I would not do to protect her."

Elizabeth folded one arm over the other. "And what if your investigations should turn up nothing at all that would discredit Mr. Bingham?"

"If the man has nothing in his past to justify my disapprobation then I will not stand in his way. That said, I have no desire to see my sister suffer further disappointment in love, but I would not be terribly upset if the man suddenly decided to go on about his business far, far from Derbyshire. My sister deserves better."

"What could be better than Georgiana spending her life with a man who loves her?"

"Spending her life with a man who loves her *and* is capable of providing for her is far better. I do not believe I am expecting too much by wishing for such an outcome."

Chapter 14

At Your Service

Whenever Wickham could, he left his wife at the Bingleys' estate and ventured to Lambton to engage in secret affairs that she did not need to know about. He had just finished one such assignation and was headed to his preferred gaming establishment when he espied an old acquaintance. He hurried across the street to where the fellow stood.

"Still destined to wherever the road leads you, my friend. No doubt it is a winding road that has led you back to this godforsaken place in the middle of nowhere."

Bingham swung about and found himself face to face with the gentleman whose acquaintance he had made the first time he was in Lambton nearly a year ago. "Indeed, it is a winding road that has brought me right back to where I ought to be."

"Ah, good fortune or a woman," said Wickham in recollection of their first meeting.

"Actually both—combined in one neat and, dare I say, comely package." Wanting to attach the forgotten name to the face, he said, "I must beg your pardon, sir. You see, I am no good at remembering names. Pray what is yours again?"

"George Wickham at your service," he replied with a slight bow. "I believe you said your name is Alston Car—"

"Bingham," the other man quickly interjected, wishing he'd never broached the subject.

Wickham's expression clouded. "No—I am certain you introduced yourself as—"

"—Much time has passed since you and I first met, sir. Moreover, let us not forget there was a fair amount of spirits consumed between the two of us. Speaking of which, pray you will join me inside this fine establishment for a drink."

Once they were settled at a table with beverages in hand, Wickham said, "Pray who is this bundle of loveliness that you spoke of before, if I may ask?"

"Unless my memory fails me, you are very acquainted with the young woman's family. Indeed, it is Miss Georgiana Darcy."

Wickham found himself almost completely at a loss for words. This—this vagabond who fancied himself a gentleman and sitting across from him dared to boast of a connection with Georgiana!

My Georgiana! Wickham silently declared. The young woman whom he had befriended when she was but a child and who was designed for him and this—this man who may have had connections but clearly no fortune of his own. Silent and grave, Wickham took a long swallow from his glass.

The other man said, "If I were a gambler, I would wager all that I own that you find my assertion troubling."

"Indeed, I do—but not for the reason you might be thinking."

"Rather than mince words, why don't you tell me the cause?"

"Well—the fact of the matter is that I would be troubled to hear any man voice the words you spoke just then. You see, Miss Darcy and I share a peculiar history. Indeed, our lives might well have been one had dark forces not intervened."

The other man laughed a little. "Pray do not tell me that she left you standing at the altar."

"Trust me; the lady had every intention of marrying me. She and I had always been close." Wickham took a sip of his drink. "Perhaps I have said too much, for I would not wish to stir up any trouble that might impede your good fortune."

"Would it ease your conscience if I were to tell you that Miss Darcy and I have already spoken of her fond attachment with another and how her brother intervened? No doubt your allusion to dark forces was meant to be Darcy himself." He picked up the bottle and capped off Wickham's glass. "I am not at all opposed to hearing your side of the story."

"As I said, I was meant to marry the young woman. I have known her all her life. As a consequence of the differences in our ages, she looked upon me more as an older brother for the best part of her youth and, indeed, in so many respects it made sense. Her father, the late Mr. Gerald Darcy, was my godfather after all. He loved me as though I were his own son."

"I fail to see where you're going with this yarn, my friend. How exactly does your being her late father's godson figure into all this? One would think that, if he loved you as much as you say he did, he would have welcomed the match."

"I have every reason to believe he would have. He loved me just that much. However, he passed away before his daughter was of an age to consider matrimony. I am afraid she was very young at the time." Wickham paused and took a sip of his drink. Resuming his former attitude, he said, "I went away from Pemberley for a time after my godfather's passing. When I had cause to return, the sweet child that I had left behind had blossomed into a young woman, and we began to renew our acquaintance.

"When I learned that she would be spending a summer in Ramsgate, I made special arrangements to visit her there. I thought it would be a fine thing to spend time with her away from her brother's disapproving presence."

Bingham's silence encouraged Wickham to continue.

"I would not say that I went there specifically to persuade her to elope with me, but—well, one thing led to another"—he arched his brow—"if you catch my meaning, and that is precisely what took place. We were that close to leaving Ramsgate for Gretna Green when her dutiful brother, the almighty Mr. Fitzwilliam Darcy, arrived in Ramsgate for a surprise visit."

His interest piqued, Bingham leaned a bit closer to hear what Wickham had to say next.

"Georgiana, not knowing of the bad blood between us and not wishing to offend a brother whom she likened to a father, shared our happy news with him soon after his arrival." Just the thought of the ensuing events cast a pall over Wickham's mood. "Darcy would not hear of it. He did everything in his power to put an end to our plans and obviously he had his way."

Here, Wickham took another sip of his drink. Wiping his mouth with the back of his hand, he continued. "Darcy accused me of doing it all to spite him, as though the inducement of thirty thousand pounds was insufficient encouragement. He thinks that much of himself. However, I dare say I got the last laugh for I ended up marrying another one of his sisters, didn't I?"

~~~

"You came home," Elizabeth said, surprised when her husband walked into her apartment.

Darcy silently commanded Elizabeth's lady's maid, who was helping with her evening toilette, to leave him alone with his wife. The woman immediately heeded his demand, laid the towel she was using to dry Elizabeth's hair aside, and quit the room. Darcy seized the towel, sat next to his wife on the bed, and resumed where the servant left off. "I told you I would do everything in my power to return to Pemberley tonight."

Elizabeth threw a cursory glance at the mantle clock. "It is so late, and you know I do not like the idea of your traveling so far in the darkness of night, even if you are accompanied by your groomsman."

"I wanted to be with you." He ceased what he was doing and kissed her on the nape of her neck. "We do not see each other nearly enough."

Elizabeth smiled lovingly at him. "This is true, my love. I do miss you exceedingly."

Resuming his earlier task, he asked, "How was your visit with the tenant wives this morning?"

"It went as well as could be expected. This morning, I spent time with Mrs. Pollard and her eldest daughter, Clarissa. The others were out and about."

Darcy pursed his lips. "What are that young woman's plans for reaching the altar?"

"I did not know you were aware of Miss Pollard's predicament."

"It is my business to know these things as master of Pemberley."

"If you know so much, perhaps you might tell her father the name of the man who is responsible for his daughter's condition so he will know how to act."

"Do you mean her father does not know with whom his daughter has been keeping company?"

"She refuses to say, which leads her poor mother to think her daughter is protecting the man's identity. She fears the gentleman may be married, perhaps even someone who is not from the vicinity."

"It is a shame. However, it is all the more reason to make certain Georgiana is not exposed to the young woman."

"I assure you Clarissa's condition is not contagious. Georgiana is in no danger in that regard."

"It is not the young lady's physical condition that concerns me, but rather the weakness of her character that has led to her condition."

"Clarissa is little more than a child, with the sweetest temperament one could imagine. Must she be condemned as lacking in good character for yielding to the temptation of the flesh? Are we not all humans, subject to the same frailties and mistakes?"

"Indeed, we are. However, that does not excuse her refusal to name the man who is responsible. That particular frailty is one of her own choosing."

"I fear she is merely afraid of the aftermath."

Elizabeth's words gave Darcy cause to think of another woman whose wantonness had led her to behave recklessly: Lydia Wickham. That young woman was someone who did not give a fig about the aftermath of what she had done. No doubt, given a second chance, she would behave no differently. His thoughts then tended to his own sister. She had almost been persuaded to throw caution to the wind and elope with George Wickham. True, she was nowhere near as silly and reckless as Lydia, but Lydia's current predicament might well be Georgiana's but for Darcy's timely intervention.

Wickham! Darcy would not have been at all surprised were he to learn that he was the man responsible for young Clarissa Pollard's plight. He knew enough about the gentleman's low propensities not to at least consider such a possibility. Wickham certainly spent enough time in the surrounding area. Darcy shook his head. Even Wickham would not sink so low as to seduce a young woman nearly two decades his junior. *Would he?* Darcy silently pondered. He shook his head to rid himself of such thoughts. Why was he wasting time thinking about his former friend when he had better things to occupy his mind—namely his lovely wife?

Such talk spurred Elizabeth's musings as well. Thoughts of the eldest Pollard daughter's situation inevitably led her to consider her own circumstances. Nearly two years of wedded bliss without an heir to show for it was no small matter. It certainly was not for want of trying.

Having completed the task of drying her hair, Darcy brushed a soft kiss across Elizabeth's shoulder.

Pulling her hair to one side, she tilted her head just so, inviting his breath's warm caresses.

Perhaps this will be the night, she considered, just as she had countless times before. "Shall we retire for the evening, my love?"

He bestowed a look that promised she'd receive no objection from him. As was their wont to do of late, she and her husband set about the task of extinguishing the candles in the maid's stead. Elizabeth was not designed for ill-humor; hence she laughed a little in silence. *Should tonight's endeavors fail to bear fruit, what sweet pleasure I shall suffer in having given it my all.* With that, she climbed into bed, leaned in the direction of her night table, and blew out the last candle.

Chapter 15

Every Intention

Darcy glared at the sanctimonious gentleman opposite him. His disgust was beyond expression. "What kind of fool are you to stand before me and speak of my sister's dowry as though it's any of your concern when I have yet to give my consent to an alliance between the two of you? You are sadly mistaken if you suppose I will ever do so now."

"Were I to share what I know about your sister's time in Ramsgate, no respectable gentleman would have her. You ought to be begging me to marry the girl; although begging in this case is entirely unnecessary as I have every intention of marrying her. All I ask for is extra compensation in light of the fact that she is damaged goods."

"My sister's reputation is above reproach."

"Come now, sir, you and I both know that is far from the truth. However, no one else need know. Double the amount of her dowry, and you shall hear not another word on this matter from me. Your sister need not know about this talk either. There is no need to upset her pretty little head with such matters."

Darcy said, "Lest you are not aware, extortion is a crime. I can see you arrested and thrown into prison for this, and then what will become of your relations?"

"Lest *you* forget, I would have my day in court, and then your sister's scandal that you've spent years covering up would be aired in a public forum. I am sure you would not want that, and you have the means of preventing it from coming about."

"I am not to be dictated to, you scoundrel. You'll get nothing from me."

"I must take it that your sister's reputation means nothing to you. What a shame. One would never know that you were the same man who took the trouble of recovering your dear wife's sister from scandal by paying all her husband's debts and obtaining his commission in Newcastle." Indeed, George Wickham had given Bingham a thorough accounting of how his marriage to Darcy's other sister had come about. The man crossed his arms before his chest. "What a shame indeed that you would go through so much trouble and expense on behalf of the one and not the other."

"If you think such blustering will persuade me, you are a bigger fool than I thought."

"A fool I may be—in your eyes—but as my sources are quite reliable, you and I both know I am not merely blustering."

Darcy said, "I am afraid I have been quite remiss in this entire affair. Perhaps I ought to be investigating you. Perhaps there is a thing or two about your own sister that you would wish to conceal from the world in general. You did say she was a widow did you not?"

Bingham's indignant expression was quite telling in view of his silence.

Darcy stood. "You need not bother to answer, for I have the means of finding out for myself. Indeed, I shall know everything there is to know about you in a matter of days and should you ever show your face again, I shall indeed know how to act. I do believe you can find your own way out, sir, and if not, I shall be happy to show you a quick route," he said, gesturing toward the window.

When his visitor was gone, Darcy wasted no time in writing a missive to his London solicitor to determine what had become of his earlier inquiries into Bingham's past. He was sealing the letter when his butler entered the room with an urgent missive in hand. Darcy accepted the letter, read it, and was stunned. The earl had suffered another fit of apoplexy. Darcy's presence was needed in Matlock post haste.

"This is grave news indeed."

"Pardon, sir?"

"My uncle's health has suffered another setback. I must leave for Matlock at once." Darcy handed the man the missive he'd just completed. "Please see that my steward handles this letter. In addition, I ask you to make my apologies to Mrs. Darcy for my abrupt departure. It cannot be helped."

Accepting the charge, the butler bowed and turned to quit the room. Darcy halted him. "On second thought, I will explain everything to my wife in a letter before I take my leave. As for the other request, it is most urgent that Mr. Howard attends it as soon as he returns from Lambton."

~~~

Bingham walked up and down the room, looking grave and anxious. His entire scheme had fallen apart, and he had no one to blame but himself.

"What was I thinking in attempting to pressure that tight-fisted Fitzwilliam Darcy to increase his sister's dowry when I was months if not weeks from fulfilling his stipulation that Georgiana and I must wait before he sanctioned our union?" He swept his fingers through his hair and threw a glance about the room. Lodging for two to keep up the appearance of a brother traveling with his sister and infant child in one of the better inns in Lambton is what had led to his rashness. The expenses had taken quite a burdensome toll on his purse.

When at first he made the offer of painting Georgiana pro bono, he truly never believed that Darcy would not offer him a single shilling as recompense for his resulting costs. Such was the way for people of Darcy's ilk Bingham had come to consider. Having never wanted for anything in their lives, they could not possibly conceive the dire financial straits of others who were less fortunate than they were.

Now he was desperate. He had to see Georgiana in private, away from her nosey companion, her inquisitive sister, and her officious brother. His patience exhausted by extreme vexation, he ceased his pacing and glared at Angelica.

"You more than anyone know how much this means to me." As much as he loved his lady, Bingham did not intend to allow her stubbornness to stand in his way. He had come too far and spent too many months devising the scheme that would be the means of him claiming his fair share of the vast Darcy family fortune.

"If I am unable to depend on you then who else might I employ? Again, I insist that you write to Georgiana Darcy on my behalf."

"I hate being a party to all this deception," Angelica cried, no doubt livid that he would ask such a thing of her.

"You know I am doing all this for you and the child."

"You keep saying that, but how can I be assured of anything, especially now when you're sending us away?"

"This separation between us is meant to be temporary, and you know it. If worse comes to worst, I may be forced to elope with the girl to Gretna Green. After the wedding takes place, you and the child will come and live with my new wife and me. So long as it is believed that you and I are half siblings, who will object to such a scheme?"

Crossing her arms in defiance, she said, "So long as you're planning to marry this girl, why can't you write to her yourself?"

"That is not the way it is done in polite society. Besides, her brother does not recognize our engagement. He has effectively banned me from stepping foot on the grounds of Pemberley. No doubt he is taking added precautions to assure that his sister and I do not have any contact with each other. This is the only way I can think of to penetrate the barrier separating Georgiana Darcy and me."

Hovering over her, he reached for the quill and dipped it into the inkwell. He then placed it between her fingers. "Now, do as I say, and write the bloody letter."

Chapter 16

A Moment Longer

"Where is Georgiana?" Elizabeth asked Mrs. Annesley upon her return from her round of morning calls on some of the tenant households.

"Is she not with you? She made it a point of mentioning to me that she would be spending the morning with you."

"She said nothing to me about her plans else I should not have left as early as I did. I think I shall have a walk about the grounds in order that I might accompany her. Georgiana has made it a habit of late to enjoy a solitary stroll along her favorite paths."

"No doubt as a consequence of enjoying your company," said the older woman knowingly. "She admires you exceedingly, and she depends on you. However, I don't suppose I need to tell you that."

"Indeed. She and I have come to depend upon each other, especially during times like these when my husband is away."

The situation of his uncle's failing health was taking its toll on Darcy, and he sometimes felt it best to remain on at the Matlock estate rather than spend an abundance of time traveling back and forth.

Elizabeth walked to the door. "What's more, I fear her spirits might be a little low what with all the tension between Mr. Darcy and Mr. Bingham. I shall attempt to cheer her up."

Before heading out, Elizabeth went to her sitting room to retrieve her favorite parasol that she'd left there days earlier. She espied a missive from her husband on her writing desk. "Oh, look! My darling Fitzwilliam must have left this here for me to find just before he took his leave," she said aloud. She did not want to put off walking out to join Georgiana a moment longer than she had to, but likewise she was eager to read her husband's missive. Knowing him as well as she did, she supposed it was a renewal of his love for her with an assurance that he would not stay away a moment longer than was necessary. She decided to read and walk at the same time.

As soon as she was at the foot of the stairs, she opened the letter:

Elizabeth, my love, I beg your pardon for the briefness of this missive. It cannot be helped. I have received news from Matlock that my uncle has suffered a serious setback in his recovery. I must leave at once. I must also tell you that Bingham and I suffered a severe impasse this afternoon that renders further association between us virtually impossible. I shall explain it all upon my return to Pemberley. Bingham is aware he is no longer welcome at Pemberley, but, as I will not be there to assure he does not attempt to circumvent my wishes, I ask that you keep an eye on the situation to make certain that Georgiana is in no danger of seeing him.

How I shall miss you, my dearest, loveliest Elizabeth. I will send word from Matlock as soon as I can.

Forever yours, FD

Reading these words added a heightened sense of urgency to Elizabeth's footsteps, not that she thought Georgiana was in any imminent jeopardy, for surely she was safe merely strolling about the lanes at Pemberley, but because Elizabeth needed to be certain of it.

~~~

A clandestine meeting with Mr. Bingham was just the thing to brighten Georgiana's dull spirits that day.

"Thank you for agreeing to see me alone, dearest Georgiana," he said after they had been walking along, sharing polite conversation for some time.

Georgiana felt as if she ought to be the one thanking him for coming to see her. It had been too long since she had the pleasure of his company, she considered. "I confess it was not easy to get away from Mrs. Annesley. I believe she has increased her vigilance of late, and I can only ascribe it to a directive from my brother to keep a sharper eye on me now that you and I have an understanding."

By Georgiana's reaction to seeing him, he was certain her brother had said nothing to her about the serious nature of their grievances against each other. In light of the fact that Darcy had banned him from setting foot on the grounds, he rightly supposed he had Darcy's propensity to keep his own counsel to thank for his being there.

"Ah, an understanding. Is that what this is?" he asked, sweeping her into his arms and pressing her body against his.

A part of her felt she ought to protest this breach of etiquette, but after the stratagems she had employed for this time alone with him, she did not know that she could without being coquettish. "I fear that is all my brother will allow it to be for now. Pray you understand."

"I fear you ought to know that things have changed between Darcy and me as a consequence of our last meeting. I am persuaded that, if left to him, you and I would never reach the altar. He has never liked me,

DEAREST, LOVELIEST ELIZABETH

and now that I have declared my intention to marry you, he likes me even less.

"Truth be told, he would be most seriously displeased were he to learn that you and I are seeing each other this way. This must be our secret for now."

Before Georgiana could fashion a response, he said, "You and I are to be husband and wife. I want to shout it out to the world. More than that, I want to do it now with no consideration for what your brother feels is best. His strongest objection to me is my lack of fortune. You and I have discussed all that, have we not? Those things mean nothing to you."

"Pray you are not suggesting that we elope. I do not believe I could do such a thing—to subject my brother to such grief and displeasure."

"No—I am not suggesting an elopement. It need never come to that. There are other ways of bringing about the happy conclusion we both long for, and once your brother finds out, he will have no choice but to accept the inevitability of our union."

"Sir—"

He placed his fingers on her lips. "Hush. I know what to do." He wetted his lips and, tracing a path to her neckline, he swept his lips along a similar course. The rise and fall of her bosom encouraged him.

"Sir—" she began again, only this time a bit more tentatively.

"Trust me," he whispered. Lowering the décolletage of her gown, he commenced admiring her—

adoring her. Her body's response was everything he knew it would be.

"Please, sir."

After circling her bosom with light strokes of his tongue, he trailed his lips about her creamy shoulders. "I intend to please you—in every way—right here and right now."

"No—no, I mean please stop."

He did not. He pressed his hard body against her soft body, giving her an indication of what was to come.

"I said stop, Mr. Bingham. Please remember yourself!"

"Your body is saying something entirely different. You are simply nervous, that is all. Do not make yourself uneasy over what we are about to do. I have a way with women. That is what you are. A woman with a woman's desires—a woman's needs.

"Your body is speaking the language of a woman desperate to come out—to throw off Society's restrictions—and I mean to be the man who sets the woman inside of you free."

"Not like this," she pleaded, attempting to push him away with both hands.

"Stop pretending you don't want this, or perchance your George Wickham never touched you like this." He swept his tongue over one taut bud and then the other. "Did he, Georgiana? Did he touch you like this?" Bingham covered her mouth with his to muddle her protests. Forcing it open to accept his hungry kisses, he commenced rather urgent, passion-filled stroking of his body against hers.

If ever she thought she wanted to be with him—to give herself to this man as a woman gave herself to her husband—she was certain she did not want it now. Not like this. It was all she could do to close her eyes, suppressing her tears, her disappointment, and her heartbreak.

Georgiana heard a loud thump! Her eyes flew open. Bingham slumped to his knees. She saw Elizabeth standing there holding a heavy branch with both hands. He stumbled to his feet and grabbed hold of Elizabeth's shoulders. He started manhandling her—shaking her.

The thought that her brother would kill Bingham for putting his hands on Elizabeth did cross Georgiana's mind but only for a second. She commenced pounding her cousin's back with clinched fists. "Leave my sister alone, you beast!" she cried with energy.

One hand tightly gripping Elizabeth's arm, the other free, he swung around and pushed Georgiana aside. She fell backward. Her head hit the sharp edge of a large rock.

The sight of his cousin lying lifelessly on the ground awakened him to what he had done. He never meant to hurt Georgiana. He rushed to her side and fell to his knees. "Look at what you've made me do," he yelled over his shoulder.

Elizabeth, seeing her sister thus, rushed to Georgiana's side and knelt beside her. "Georgiana—Georgiana!" she cried. "Georgiana, wake up!"

"Look at what you forced me to do. It did not have to come to this. She and I were to be married."

"My husband will have your head for this." She tore her eyes from Bingham's to her unconscious sister. Her sister's bloodstained dress took her breath away. Tears welled up inside her as she placed her hand on Georgiana's face. "Please, Georgiana, please do not leave us."

Bingham seized Elizabeth's arm and pulled her to her feet. "You're coming with me!"

She fought back. "Unhand me at once. I must attend my sister." Her struggle in vain, Elizabeth yelled out. "Help!"

He put his hand over her mouth. "Quiet! Do not force me to lay another hand on you."

She bit his hand with all her might, forcing him to pull it away. "Someone help us!" Elizabeth shouted at the top of her lungs. "Someone help us, please!"

Bingham tore off his cravat and stuffed it into her mouth. "I said be quiet." He lifted Elizabeth, threw her over his shoulder as though she were merely a sack of wheat, and scampered off to where he had tethered his horse.

Chapter 17

Pursue the Matter

Several letters awaited Darcy upon his arrival from Matlock that afternoon. Only one of them was of concern—the one from his man in London who was charged with investigating Bingham's past. After tearing it open and hastily reading it, Darcy slammed his fist on the table. "That lying scoundrel," he said aloud. "His half-sister indeed." He now understood why Bingham had kept her tucked away in Lambton rather than allow her to accompany him to Pemberley. *That woman is his paramour! What was he about in introducing her to Georgiana and Elizabeth as his half-sister?*

I must see Georgiana at once. Although I do not relish the idea of breaking her heart, she needs to know the truth. Darcy quit his study in search of his sister. He had not gotten far before espying her paid companion.

"Mrs. Annesley, you are just the person I need to speak with."

She curtsied. "Welcome home, sir. I pray your uncle, the Earl of Matlock, is in much-improved health."

Remembering himself, Darcy bowed slightly. "Indeed, he is. I thank you."

"How can I be of service, sir?"

"I need to speak with my sister, immediately. Will you tell me where I might find her?"

"Miss Darcy went for a walk around the grounds."

"Alone?" Darcy interrupted.

"Indeed, I came to learn that she had set out alone. At first, I was under the impression she was with Mrs. Darcy. When Mrs. Darcy returned from her visit with one of the tenant families, I learned that she and Miss Darcy had not been together. It was then that Mrs. Darcy said she would join Miss Darcy on her walk."

"How long ago did my wife leave to meet my sister?"

"I am afraid I cannot say with specificity, but I imagine it's been hours. I know that they have yet to return for Miss Darcy and I had another engagement. I know how the two ladies so enjoy long, rambling walks, which I suppose must be Miss Darcy's excuse for foregoing our plans."

After taking his leave of Mrs. Annesley, Darcy decided what he needed to say to his sister could not wait, and thus he set out to meet the ladies. He had been walking for nearly a quarter of an hour when he espied his sister moving slowly in his direction. He raced to her and reached her just in time. Dazed and confused, she collapsed in his arms. Dropping to his knees to better support her, he touched her face. "Georgiana!"

She was lifeless.

"Georgiana, my sweet—" He brushed her tangled hair from her face and kissed her forehead. "Georgiana, pray open your eyes," he pleaded.

She opened them a little and spoke faintly. Cradling her in his arms, Darcy leaned closer. Bloodstains marred his sleeve.

"Elizabeth," she whispered.

"What about Elizabeth?"

"Mr. Bingham—she tried to stop him."

"Bingham did this to you? Where is Elizabeth?"

"She hit him. He was angry. He attacked her." Her voice fell silent again. Her eyes closed.

Darcy's heart skipped a beat. "My wife! I must find my wife," he said, the sound of his voice like that of a stranger.

"I'm sorry," he heard his sister say.

"Hush. Do not try to speak, dearest. I will find Elizabeth."

His sister in his arms, he stood and hurried back to the manor house. He handed her over to the butler. "My sister is severely wounded. Get her to her room and summon the physician, now!"

Without delay, he went to his study and exhaled a sigh of relief that his steward was there. "I fear a terrible fate has befallen Mrs. Darcy. I have no time to explain. Organize a party to search the grounds. I will return to the path along the river where I found my sister and begin looking for my wife there."

A knock at the door drew both men's attention. In walked one of the footmen. "What is it?" Darcy asked.

"Sir, I—I..."

"Go on, man. I have no time to waste!"

The footman commenced explaining the reason for his being there. He spoke of having seen someone on horseback racing away from Pemberley Woods while he was walking. What's more, the man was not alone. It looked to the footman as though there was someone slung over his lap. The frantic rider had set off in the direction of Lambton. Darcy knew exactly how to act!

When Darcy arrived at the Lambton inn where Bingham and his family were staying, the innkeeper informed him that the Bingham party had quit the establishment first thing that morning.

"I watched as the young woman cradling the babe was handed into the coach."

"What of the gentleman?"

"He did not accompany them. By the manner of their parting, I was under the distinct impression he was seeing them off specifically. In fact, he returned and had a drink at his usual table before heading out a half hour or so later."

Darcy looked in the direction of the other man's gaze. There sat his old nemesis—Wickham. Suspecting the worst, he tore over to him. Darcy reached across the table and seized Wickham by the throat. "If I find out that you have a hand in my wife's abduction, I will kill you."

Wickham's mouth fell open. "What are you saying? Has Elizabeth been taken?"

"You dare deny knowing it!"

"Elizabeth is my sister, man! I care for her deeply. Why would I wish to harm her?"

"Do you also deny telling Alston Bingham about your thwarted plans for my sister?"

"Alston Bingham?" Wickham twisted his lips, pretending to query his memory. He shook his head. "I never heard of the man."

"Liar!" Darcy spat, releasing his former friend with violent force. He had to have been lying. Who else would have shared intelligence of the Ramsgate affair but Wickham?

Wickham stumbled backward and landed awkwardly in his chair. Composing himself, he said, "Well— what if I do know the gentleman? What if I did tell him the things you accuse me of telling him?"

Darcy's temper he dared not vouch for by now. "Do not play games with me, Wickham."

"This man you speak of—this Alston Bingham—if that's even his name," Wickham began, still convinced he knew the man as Carter, "I have met him before—in this very establishment. He said he and Georgiana were betrothed. Surely you will agree a future husband ought to know such a thing about the woman he intends to wed."

"That fool's name *is* Alston Bingham. He is behind my wife's disappearance. When did you last see him?"

"I saw him little over an hour or so ago. He was behaving very strangely, I might add. I espied him nearby an old, abandoned building just on the outskirts of town. I called out to him, but he slipped inside without acknowledging me."

"Why did you not pursue the matter?"

"Who am I to say the fellow was not involved in secret affairs of some kind?"

"Take me there," Darcy demanded.

"Why should I do that? I am not looking for any trouble."

He pierced his adversary with a disbelieving glare. "This is my wife's life, man—the sister whom you professed to caring about mere moments ago." Darcy seized Wickham again. "If something happens to Elizabeth, it will be on your head. Heaven help you then."

"What can you possibly do to me that you have not already done?"

"Trust me, Wickham; you do not want to know!"

When the two of them arrived at the old, abandoned building, Darcy said, "I shall handle things from here." Further assistance from Wickham was the last thing he wanted. The idea of having to rely upon the scoundrel whose loose lips had been the catalyst for this horrible situation bothered Darcy more than a little. However, his loathing toward his former friend was nothing in comparison to his desperation to discover his wife and bring her home safely. On the other hand, he supposed that, had Wickham not unwittingly provided the means for Alston Bingham's attempt at extortion, the latter's true character might not have been revealed. Darcy shook his head. Of course, there was the matter of the man's mistress. What manner of degenerate had he allowed into his sister and his wife's life?

"Do you not want my help?" Wickham beseeched. "Who is to say what awaits you on the other side of that door."

"I never knew you cared."

"I don't give a fig about what happens to you, but I do care about my sister."

"I wish you would stop referring to my wife as such."

"It's true, and you have yourself to thank for that, do you not?"

"Silence, you fool! If you insist upon being of further service, perhaps you might alert the town constable to what is afoot. Pray have a care in returning with reinforcements. I would not wish to make Bingham desperate."

Chapter 18

A Gentleman

Just as darkness had fallen over the town of Lambton, so did complete darkness befall Darcy moments after he made way into the rundown building. Upon opening his eyes, he could not account for the previous passage of time. All he knew was his head pounded, he was bound to a wooden chair, and foul water was dripping from his face.

Darcy commenced a valiant struggle to free himself. *Am I alone? Has my assailant fled? How long have I been tied up like this?* Such were the questions racing through his mind.

"Where is my wife, Bingham?" Darcy demanded when the severely disheveled man came into view with a bucket in his hand.

"Your wife is perfectly safe—for now," he said, tossing the empty bucket against the wall.

"If you've harmed my wife, I will see you twisting by your neck from a rope."

"Be quiet, will you? I must determine what to do next. I had not planned for you to come here." He combed his fingers through his unkempt hair. "If nothing else, you have saved me the trouble of fashioning a ransom note. Now the question remains of who will pay to secure both of your freedom."

"You fool! Your plan is not very well thought out."

His eyes wild, Bingham looked at the other man in dismay. "Of course my plan is not well thought out. What do you think I am? Some sort of criminal?"

"First, you attempted to blackmail me. Now you have resorted to kidnapping. If not a criminal, what would you call yourself?"

"I am a man who is violently in love!"

"In love," Darcy repeated mockingly. "Who are you in love with? Your paramour—your *so-called* half-sister?"

Panic overspread Bingham's face. "You know nothing about her!"

"Did you really suppose your lies would not come to light?"

"Quiet! I meant *your* sister. She and I were to be married. Your darling wife happened upon us at the wrong time. She misunderstood what she saw." He slapped his hands on either side of his head and shook it. "How is Georgiana? Pray tell me she is unharmed."

"How dare you ask about my sister?"

"She is my own flesh and blood. She has come to mean a great deal to me!"

Darcy spat on the floor in response to Bingham's contention. "What happened to you? You boast of being a Darcy. A true Darcy would never stoop so low."

"My usurped birthright is what happened to me," the younger man exclaimed.

"Your birthright? How dare you suggest that decades past fortunes in life have been the means of reducing you to this desperate caricature of a man? One who would go from extortion to kidnapping in order to get what you want."

"Listen to you, giving yourself airs. What if our family's history had been different? What if *my* grandfather had been the elder son? What if all that you boast of being your own, merely by circumstance of the order of someone's birth, had redound to a different branch of our family tree? What if you enjoyed the lineage of a gentleman yet were forced to endure the hardships afforded the common man? But you wouldn't know anything about that would you, Darcy? You have been handed everything you ever wanted, haven't you?"

Darcy stealthily continued loosening the ropes binding his hands. "Not everything," he said in a hushed voice.

As he had hoped, his captor drew closer. "What was that you said?"

Darcy grabbed the young man by the neck with one hand and pounded him in his face with the other. "I said, not everything."

Bingham slumped, unconscious, to the floor. Darcy scrambled to untie his legs and he used his former bindings to tie the younger man to the empty chair.

Frantically, he looked around the room. There was but one door other than the one he had entered. *Pray to God my Elizabeth is on the other side.*

He kicked the door open. The room was large. The lighting was poor. As best Darcy could make out, old work tools, spare carriage parts and the like lay haphazardly organized all about. What a wretched place indeed for his beloved wife, if she were even there. A barely perceptible thump drew his attention.

Is it my wife? He hurried in the direction of the sound, and then was momentarily taken aback when a rat the size of a small feline scurried past his feet. What he had heard was more urgent than an inconvenienced rat and deserved closer inspection. Clearing a path, he saw what appeared to be a large sack. Closer inspection revealed it was no sack at all. It was Elizabeth. Bound by her hands and her feet, she lay completely still.

Thank heavens his prayers were answered. Darcy sank to his knees beside her. "Elizabeth, my love—"

Taking her in his arms, he removed the cloth gag from her mouth. Her hair in utter disarray, her clothing badly tattered and soiled, Elizabeth did not respond.

Darcy cradled her to his chest and kissed her atop her head. "Pray open your eyes, my love."

She awakened to his plea this time. Her eyes bloodshot from her tears, she said, "Georgiana? Is she—?"

"Elizabeth, my love," he cried, holding her tighter. "Georgiana is at Pemberley. You need not worry about her."

"But," she began, her voice strained and weak. "She fell—hit her head."

Darcy kissed his wife's face and commenced removing the binding on her hands and next her feet. "Are you injured, my love? Did he harm you?"

"My head," she said, swallowing, "it hurts."

Darcy traced his fingers along her face and about her scalp in search of possible life-threatening injuries. Finding none, he prayed silent thanks. He stood, lifting his wife in his arms. "Let me carry you away from this godforsaken place to Pemberley where you will receive proper attention, my love."

"Pray how is Georgiana?" Elizabeth moaned weakly.

"Georgiana is safe. Both of you are safe."

~~~

Still rather shaken and utterly consumed with the notion of having been horribly ill-used, the only thing Elizabeth wanted to do by the time she and Darcy returned to Pemberley was to see her sister Georgiana. She suffered more than a little guilt that she had not seen through Mr. Bingham's well-honed facade of gentlemanly airs. The man was nothing more than an opportunist whose desperation had incited him to commit outrageous crimes. She was glad that he had not inflicted more pain upon her innocent sister. Georgiana thought kindly of everyone and did not deserve such callous treatment. Elizabeth could hardly countenance the thought of what might have happened had she chanced upon her sister and Bingham a moment too late.

Heaven forbid what might have taken place had I chosen a different path when seeking out Georgiana earlier, Elizabeth ruminated.

Georgiana was peacefully sleeping when Elizabeth entered the room. The nurse who sat by the bed keeping watch over the younger woman quietly assured Elizabeth that all was well before standing and leaving. Elizabeth took the vacated seat. Placing her hand on Georgiana's, Elizabeth closed her eyes and prayed in gratitude. First, to have suffered a broken heart because of Wickham's deception, and now, to have been a victim of her cousin's debauchery was a weighty load for a young lady to shoulder. The former was a man whom she had known and trusted for the better part of her life. The latter was a man whom she had revered as her own flesh and blood. Elizabeth knew her sister would soon recover from the physical wounds from that day's ordeal. As for her ability to recover from the emotional bruises, Elizabeth was rather less certain.

A tiny tear escaped Elizabeth's eye, and then another until her weeping would not be suppressed. Hers were tears of heartbreak on her sister's behalf over all she had endured and would surely continue to suffer for the weeks and months ahead. Hers were also tears of relief mixed with gratitude. Georgiana was safe from harm.

Georgiana began stirring. Opening her eyes and seeing Elizabeth, she gently squeezed her sister's hand. Her voice strained, she whispered, "Elizabeth."

Elizabeth wiped away her tears. Standing, she leaned forward and embraced Georgiana while taking special care not to disturb her bandaged wounds.

"I am sorry," Georgiana said.

Elizabeth gingerly sat on the bed and took her sister by the hand. "No, my dear, you have no reason to apologize."

"I was foolish. I should never have agreed to meet my cousin alone. None of this would have happened. You would never have met with harm."

"Pray, let us not ascribe blame at such a time as this, else I shall find my actions wanting as well."

"You could not have known that my cousin was not the man whom he pretended to be."

Elizabeth shrugged. "No, I could not have known and neither could you."

Georgiana tried to sit up straight, but Elizabeth silently persuaded her to lie still. "I shall leave you alone to rest."

"I must know what happened. The last thing I remembered was Mr. Bingham putting his hands on you and pushing me away when I tried to stop him," the younger woman cried with energy.

"As you can see, my dear, I am perfectly alright. Pray, do not trouble yourself with worrying on my behalf. However, I shall fret exceedingly if you do not rest."

"Will you stay with me for a while longer?"

Elizabeth tenderly caressed her sister's hand. "Of course I will, Georgiana. I shall remain by your side for as long as you need me."

~~~

Some days later, Georgiana, a much-recovered young lady, went in search of her brother. At least she had healed physically. Evidence of her lingering heartache was written plainly all over her face. Being defiled by the man whom she had been eager to give her heart to completely was something she would not soon forget.

She found Darcy sitting alone in the parlor, reading. Slowly, she walked to where he sat, and claimed the empty space beside him. "Can you ever forgive me, Brother?"

Closing his book, he took her hand, raised it to his lips, and kissed it. "Forgive you? I love you."

"Oh, but you must think I am terribly stupid. I wanted so desperately to believe in my cousin's goodness when you were not fooled for a second."

"Georgiana, you must not be too severe on yourself. You are a warm and trusting creature by nature, whereas it is my obligation to be suspect. I do not think I will ever truly suppose any man deserves you. You are my little sister."

"You see me as such, but I am not a little girl."

Darcy embraced his sister. Of course she was not a little girl. He must remember not to think or speak of her in such terms. She had endured so much strife through the years. Hers had not been an ideal life, what with the loss of their parents. His young sister was not merely missing a mother's love; she was missing a father's love as well. He was meant to be both a father and brother to her. Was such a thing even possible? Not for the first time, he wondered how his sister might have fared had his father named his aunt Lady Catherine as her guardian. No doubt it was what his mother would have done—named her only sister to care for her underage daughter.

No—my father got it right. No one is better able to protect my sister than I am and my father knew it.

"Brother," she said, "will I ever find the joy I seek? Or will the kind of love I long for always turn out to be the wrong kind of love for me?"

"Georgiana, you must trust that the right man will come along. There is no need to be in a hurry.

What's more, you must not allow what happened to affect your expectations of what the future holds."

Elizabeth entered the room and observed the siblings sitting together. Not wishing to interrupt such a tender moment that perhaps was meant to be private, she halted. As she was about to turn and quit the room, Darcy looked up. He waved her over to where he and Georgiana sat.

She went to him and accepted his outstretched hand. Seeing this, Georgiana dabbed at her eyes and prepared to stand. Darcy said, "No—stay. Elizabeth, sit with us." He adjusted his position to accommodate his wife. Embracing the ladies in his arms, he said, "There is room enough here—" he kissed his sister atop her head "—in my life—" he kissed his wife's face "—and in my heart for both of you."

Chapter 19

Happy News

Darcy sat across the table from Wickham. "What is so urgent that you insisted upon seeing me at this hour?"

"It appears the time has come for my lovely wife and me to return to our home. I had not heard a word from you, and, quite frankly, I had expected it."

After the waiter attending them filled both gentlemen's glasses with brandy, left the decanter on the table at Wickham's behest and was gone, Darcy reached into his pocket and retrieved a small package. It contained a token of his gratitude for Wickham's part in Elizabeth's recovery. He slid it across the table. "Is this what you want?"

Wickham untied the package. His eyes opened wide. "I say it is a good start."

"You'll get no more from me, you fool."

"And so you say. Nevertheless, I thank you, my old friend. This shall go a long way toward assuring the comfort of what I hope will be an olive branch to you and your family."

"Pray what is that supposed to mean?"

"Have you not heard? My lovely wife is about to make me a proud papa," Wickham replied with a self-satisfied air.

Darcy laughed a little. "I suppose I ought to be congratulating you."

"It is the proper thing to do in such cases as this."

"Pray that is the only fruit of your loins conceived of late."

Having upended his first drink, Wickham poured himself another. "What are you accusing me of now?"

Darcy arched his brow. "Does the name Miss Clarissa Pollard mean anything to you?"

Wickham studied his hand intently. Brushing his thumb over his nails, he then looked at his former friend. "I cannot say that it does."

"Perhaps you want to take another moment to think about it."

"Come now, Darcy. Even you can see the futility of your question. Were I to recall every young woman of my acquaintance, you and I would be here all night. So long as you are providing the drinks, I for one would not object, but I imagine you are in a hurry to return to your lovely wife's side."

Darcy contented himself with Wickham's nonchalant assertion. Even if Wickham were the person responsible for Miss Pollard's predicament, the last thing any of them needed was for that bit of truth to come out. Having vowed to do what he could to lessen the Pollard family's woes, he decided to leave it at that. As for the matter of Darcy's being in a hurry to return to his wife's side, Wickham was absolutely correct. He could scarcely wait to see her and hold her in his arms again.

Finished with his drink, he said, "Your little olive branch notwithstanding, you're still not welcome at Pemberley."

"I would expect no less of you, Darcy. You and your irrevocably good opinion once lost and all else aside, tell me this: what happened to your cousin after you managed to get the charges dropped against him? I still am not certain how you managed to bring that about—but, then again, money is power."

Bingham had been right about one thing. Darcy would never have permitted the reason for his crimes to be aired in a public trial. Georgiana had suffered enough. Contrary to what the public might be led to believe, she was not a ruined woman. She was a young lady whose affectionate heart rendered her a bit too trusting, but she was not without hope. Georgiana's future was bright. Darcy would make certain of that.

"Do not trouble yourself with worry over how I brought it all about."

"Do you mean bought?" Wickham taunted.

Leaning back in his chair and crossing his arms over his chest, Darcy said, "What happened with Bingham is none of your concern."

"Oh, I must beg to differ. I truly wish to know in case I ever find myself in a similar situation as that fellow and need to avail myself of your generosity."

Wickham's goading recalled Darcy to the last time he had extended similar generosity on the former's behalf. He would never have lifted a finger in that regard had it not been for his desire to protect Elizabeth's family from certain ruination and shame. He could not deny he might help Wickham again should it ever come to that. On the other hand, there was no saying that he would. It all depended on the offense itself and its effect on his family.

"Bingham is a coward who committed a most egregious act against the women I love, and so I suppose the two of you have that in common. However, the thing he has going for him—two things really—that you do not is that he is a Darcy by blood, and he has the potential to make something of himself. He shall have a chance to do so when the slow-moving boat that he now finds himself on, along with his so-called family and his *masterpiece*, reaches the shores of America."

~~~

A day or so later, Elizabeth was walking along with her mind busily engaged in reading a letter from Jane. The purpose of Jane's letter was threefold. First, she wrote of her happiness that the Wickhams were finally taking their leave of her home. In mere days, the Bingleys would have their house to themselves. Miss Bingley, having withstood all she could of Lydia and her dear Wickham, had taken it upon herself to get her own establishment in London. Never again would she risk exposing herself to the likes of the Wickhams. Jane had jokingly remarked on what an unexpected benefit that particular situation wrought. Without saying too much, Jane also hinted that, should the Wickhams return, there would be an addition to their party—a most welcome addition.

Jane expressed, in no uncertain terms, that she and Bingley shared a similar fate and she could not be happier. Her greatest wish was that Elizabeth and Darcy might soon convey the same happy news.

Looking up from her letter, Elizabeth was delighted to see her handsome husband standing in the path just up ahead. She tucked her letter into her pocket and hurried toward him. Meeting him half way, she greeted him with outstretched hands. "I thought you were going to Matlock to visit your uncle."

"I had intended to do so, indeed, and I was well on my way when I was overtaken by an express rider with the news that my uncle had made other plans."

This intelligence met with Elizabeth's pleasure exceedingly. "It sounds as though he is well on his way to a full recovery."

"Indeed. It is just as I said from the start; my uncle is stubborn enough to outlive us all."

"May we all live on for hundreds of years to come," she said jokingly, knowing such a prospect could not possibly unfold.

Darcy laughed a little. Having accepted his wife's proffered hands, he raised them to his lips. He kissed one and then the other. "Your spirits are much improved today, my love."

"Indeed. I was just reading a letter from Jane. She shared the happy news that there will be a new addition to her family."

"Do you mean to say Jane is with child? Capital! I know how much Charles has looked forward to this."

"It appears that Jane's child will have a cousin who is close to it in—"

"—Ah," Darcy interrupted, "would this be by way of the Wickhams? George hinted as much when he and I last spoke in Lambton. Of course, I did not believe a word of what he had to say, which is why I said nothing of it before. I rather supposed he was merely attempting to insinuate himself into our good graces."

"He spoke the truth, for Jane said as much. However, when I speak of Jane's child having a cousin who is close to it, I speak of more than of age, but rather proximity." Freeing one of her hands, she rested it on her stomach and gave her husband a knowing smile.

His eyes brightened and a hopeful expression swept across his countenance. "Truly, Elizabeth?"

She nodded. "Indeed. The doctor confirmed what I have been long hoping for just this morning. Are you happy, Mr. Darcy?"

He took his wife into his arms and kissed her lips. Breaking the kiss, he gazed into her eyes. "Yes, my love. I am the happiest man alive."

Some hours later, Darcy and Elizabeth joined hands and walked to the balcony to admire nature's picturesque view. At length, they commenced doing what lovers did in such situations as this. The setting sun, the gentle touch of his lips against her skin, and the intoxicating scent of him all combined to evoke the sweet and tender melody of her heartstrings, and she knew she was blessed.

If only everyone near and dear to us could feel this way, she wistfully mused. Her mind drifted to her sister Georgiana and their recent heartfelt talks. She thought of the pain the younger woman was suffering owing to her badly abused trust and the ensuing disappointed hopes. Elizabeth had endeavored to remind her sister that what happened with her cousin was not Georgiana's fault and most of all, she must not be afraid to one day surrender her heart again. Elizabeth prayed rather than knew her words made a difference.

"We have so much for which to be thankful. My greatest wish is for Georgiana to know the kind of happiness we enjoy as well," Elizabeth said.

"She will in time."

"Then you do not believe this latest experience has dampened her enthusiasm?"

"My sister is nothing if not resilient. True, she is disappointed in love now, but, in time, she will put all this into its proper perspective."

"I pray you are correct. When such a day comes, so long as you give her leave to make her own choices, I shall have no cause to complain."

"When have I ever been able to deny you your pleasure in anything?" Reflecting upon his own blessings for a moment, he said, "You make me very happy and for that I am exceedingly grateful."

"Indeed. With that said, would I seem too terribly selfish were I to thank you for all you have given me? You have made my life a paradise."

"No—you are not selfish at all. However, if you will allow, I believe I ought to be thanking you—for giving me what might be my heir, for making my house a home, for standing with me and enduring every obstacle that threatened to tear us apart." Holding his wife tenderly in his arms, he said, "Thank you for your wit, your grace, and your charm." He rested his forehead against hers. "Most of all, my dearest, loveliest Elizabeth," he whispered, "thank you for your love."

Visit Two Centuries Beyond Pemberley

and

Discover Other Books by P. O. Dixon

bit.ly/TwoCenturiesBeyondPemberley

Audiobooks Available Also

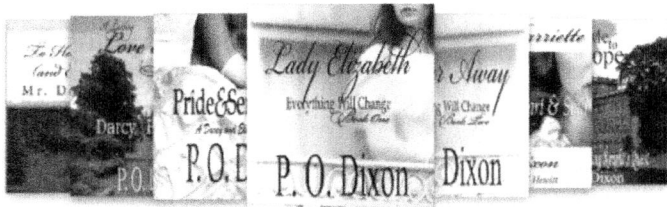

The Author

P. O. Dixon is a writer as well as an entertainer. Historical England and its days of yore fascinate her. She, in particular, loves the Regency period with its strict mores and oh so proper decorum. Her ardent appreciation of Jane Austen's timeless works set her on the writer's journey. Dixon delights in weaving diverting tales of gallant gentlemen on horseback and the women they love. Visit podixon.com and find out more about Dixon's writing endeavors.

Connect with the Author Online

Twitter: @podixon

Facebook: facebook.com/podixon

Website: podixon.com

Newsletter: bit.ly/SuchHappyNews

Email: podixon@podixon.com

Printed in Great Britain
by Amazon

16019963R00120